Froggy's

Little

Brother.

BY

BRENDA,

Author of "Nothing to Nobody."

𝕎ith Illustrations by Cas.

CONTENTS.

———◆———

FROGGY'S LITTLE BROTHER.

CHAPTER I.

THE BETTER LAND.

IN the neighbourhood of Shoreditch, a part of the East End of London inhabited mostly by very poor, hard-working people, and seldom visited by the grand West End folk, there lived some years ago a father and mother and two little boys. The father had a Punch and Judy show, which supported the family, and kept them all employed except little Benny, the baby boy. While the father was showing off Punch inside the green curtain, and making those funny nasal noises which all London children know so well, the mother used to stand by with Benny asleep in her arms, watching that no inquisitive ones should come too close, and peep into the mysteries behind the green curtain. Then Froggy, the elder boy, who was not much more

A

than a baby either in size, but was very wise beyond his years, used to stand by the drum, keeping shrewd watch on all the windows from which people could see the performance, so that when it was ended, and the time came for collecting the money, he could tell mother exactly where to go for it. This little boy's real name was Tommy, but his father had always called him *Froggy*, because he was so often cold, and croaked sometimes when he had a cough, like those little creatures who live in the ditches, and have such very wide mouths and large goggle eyes.

It was a very hard life that these poor people led. Every morning they used to sally forth from their home in Shoreditch to go to wealthier neighbourhoods, where people could afford the luxury of Punch. No matter what the weather was, whether hail, rain, snow, or sunshine, in summer or winter, they went; and, as a rule, I believe, the worse the weather was, the richer they returned at night. On rainy, bad days, when the little children living in the squares and terraces towards the rich West End could not go out, as soon as they heard the familiar sound of the drum, and the shrill "Oy! oy!" coming round the corner, they would run off, and entreat mammas and papas and indulgent grandmammas, to let them set up Punch *just* this once, as it was so dull indoors, and they had nothing to amuse them! And this generally ended in two or three little beaming faces appearing at the dining-room window, nodding "Yes!" frantically to the Punch and Judy party, who were standing out in the cold and rain waiting anxiously for the first nod as a signal to let down the green curtain, and to open the mysterious box. Then out would come Punch with his funny nose and red cheeks, and the Judy, and the beadle, and doctor, and ghost, and all the rest of the things.

It was a sad sight sometimes to see the family returning home after the day's work was done;— the father in front, carrying the Punch show, now and then walking, alas! very unsteadily, from the effects of a visit to the public-house;—and behind— saddest of all—the poor mother, with her thin face and consumptive cough, carrying little Benny, and cheering on Froggy at her side, who would often look up into her face and say—

"I are so tired, Mudder! I wish I was little, like Benny, to be carried!"

"Froggy, be good, and walk out brave, and he shall soon have his nice supper, and enjoy it ever so!" the mother would say soothingly; and at the sound of her voice Froggy gained fresh courage, and would never complain again till they reached the place in Shoreditch which these poor people called home.

Home did they call it? Ah well! home is home whatever it is like, isn't it? But theirs was a peculiarly wretched one;—only a very bare garret, at the top of a dark, dingy house, the

upper part of which was scorched and blackened
from the effects of a fire, which had occurred several
years ago, on the opposite side of the way, and
which had damaged more or less all the panes of
glass in the neighbouring windows. These windows afforded a considerable amount of ventilation,
which was felt severely by the occupants on bitter
winter nights; and in consideration of this fact,
the landlady, who was given to drinking, and could
never make up her mind to spend the money to
have fresh glass put in, had consented to let the
garret to the Punch and Judy man and his family
at a very reduced rate. The careful mother had
pasted sheets of brown paper over some of these
broken panes, and stopped up small holes in others
with such rags as she could spare;—even *rags*, my
little readers, are precious things in some homes!
On Saturdays she always tried to come home an
hour or two earlier, that she might clean up and
tidy this desolate room for Sunday; for she loved
God's holy Sabbath, and she liked to have all clean
and bright to welcome the resting-day of the week—
God's own good gift to the toilers of this world, which
only He could have given them as their *birthright*,
however their fellow-men may sometimes rob them
of it. Do we ever think enough of its preciousness
to weary workers when sometimes Sundays are
called *dull* days in luxurious homes by people who
are idle, or only idly busy, all the week?

One night, late in December, there was a sadder

pilgrimage homewards than there had ever been
before, and one which little Froggy will never forget,
even when he grows up and becomes a man. It had
been raining and snowing all day at the West End, and
though they had been trudging about the streets and
squares as usual, they had done very little business,
and were returning with scarcely any more money in
their pockets than they had started out with in the
morning. The father, sullen and angry as he was
apt to be when he had done a bad day's business,
stalked doggedly on in front with the Punch and
Judy show, making no room for anybody, but making
everybody make room for him ; and following behind
in the pitiless rain, with their clothes hanging wet and
limp about them, came the poor mother with Froggy
and Benny. Benny was asleep as usual, with a smile
on his little white face as he nestled close to his
mother, evidently in happy oblivion of the dark,
rainy world through which he was being carried. But
not so with Froggy ; he was wide awake, and fully
alive to everything that was going on around him.
He could not tell what it was, but he felt certain there
was something terribly wrong with mother to-night.
So deep was his conviction of this, that he never once
thought of looking up into her face, as he generally
did, to tell her he was so tired, and to ask her if they
would soon be home. He felt that somehow *he* must
be the comforter to-night.

"What made mother look so ghastly pale when
they passed under the gas-lamps ? Why did she

totter and walk so crooked? What made her hold Benny so loose in her arms? Why didn't she speak to him? And why did she linger so far behind, and never hurry on to keep up with father and the Punch?" Froggy kept asking himself these questions over and over again as he walked silently beside her, keeping pace with her unequal steps, and holding a little bit of her gown. At last a terrible thought flashed across him, which filled his childish heart with infinite pain and consternation. Mother had gone into a public-house with father he remembered, when he had been left outside to look after the Punch. Was it possible, he wondered, that mother could have taken something then that was making her walk like this? The suspicion was too intolerable to keep to himself, and Froggy, looking up into her face with scared anxious eyes, called out—

"Mudder! Mudder, dear! haven't you been and gone and taken something too strong to drink, like Fader does?"

The voice of Froggy seemed to rouse the poor woman with a start.

"Oh no, Froggy!" she answered with a deep sob in her voice. "I'm only very, very ill! I don't know as how I shall get home, Froggy."

"Give me Benny, Mudder," said Froggy gently, ready to cry at the thought of having said anything unkind to Mother. "I've often carried 'im, that I have—he's not none too big for me;" and he stopped before her, and put out his arms for Benny.

The mother tried to speak, but her pale lips only trembled, and she let the tiny burden fall loosely from her own into Froggy's arms. Ah! Froggy knew then how ill she must be to give up Benny so quietly, for on no other occasion had she ever let him carry his little brother through the streets, for fear his head should get knocked in the crowd, or that Froggy would tumble down; for Froggy, after all, was only a few sizes larger than Benny!

Relieved of Benny, the mother seemed to get on somewhat better. Every now and then she would stop and lean against a lamp-post or a door-way to recover her breath, which she was drawing very quickly, as if it were a great labour to her, or she would pause for a moment with her hand on Froggy's shoulder in the middle of the street, as if she were trying to steady herself. Froggy continually encouraged her, using the same words that she had so often used to him when they were going home.

"We are in Soreditch now," he said once, as she faltered more and seemed to grow weaker. "Only a very few steps more, and you shall be home, Mudder!"

Froggy did not know how very near his mother was to the end of the longest journey that ever man, woman, or child can take, and which ends to the good and true ones of this earth in that Eternal Home beyond the skies, about which little Froggy as yet did not understand much.

"Please, God, help Mudder home!" prayed poor

Froggy aloud, as the rain came down in torrents, and the wind came cutting round the corner of the dark street. " I wish Fader hadn't run on so quick, and then I could a taken Punch, and he could a helped Mudder; but I can't see him nowhere!"

Fancy that poor little bit of a boy, already staggering under the light weight of Benny, thinking he could manage the Punch show as well! But Froggy's idea of the weights he could carry, and the things he could do at a pinch, were quite boundless.

After much toiling and stopping, they reached the house in Shoreditch at last. God had heard Froggy's prayer, you see, though it had been such a short one, spoken to Him from the crowded bustling street. Froggy opened the door of the dismal house, with its blackened front and broken windows, and ran up as quickly as he could to the top garret, where his father had arrived before them, and told him " to come down quick, and help Mudder upstairs, for she was fainty-like in the passage, and couldn't get upstairs nohow !" The father obeyed the call at once, and went down to his wife, whom he carried upstairs, and laid tenderly enough on the straw mattress which was her bed. He thoughtfully took off her wet shawl and gown, and her sodden boots, and wrapped her round in the one warm blanket which they possessed. She had been a good help-mate to him,—a simple-minded, loving, Christian woman ; and the thought that he might lose her filled him with untold dread. She had often been " fainty-

like " before, but he had never seen her look like this.
She was the first generally to bustle about and get
the supper, and make everything comfortable (as far,
at least, as it ever lay in her power to do so) when
they returned to their garret at the end of the day.
She would first minister to her husband's wants, like
a faithful and good wife, and then tend little Froggy
and Benny, and make them almost forget the rain
and the snow, and the toil of the day that was over.
But to-night things were wofully changed. She lay
quite still on the mattress, with her eyes closed, asking
no questions, saying no word, and apparently unconscious of all that was going on around her. The
father kindled a fire and made some tea, and told
Froggy to feed and undress Benny and put him to
bed, as mother wouldn't be able to do it to-night.

Benny's bed was always a matter of preparation,
for where do you think he slept ? Why, on the top
of the box which contained the Punch and the Judy,
and the coffin, and the rest of the things! A little
mattress and bolster were laid upon it, and there
Benny used to sleep, and suck his fists, and dream
his happy baby dreams, as peacefully as any little
prince in his cradle! It was a matter of constant
speculation with Froggy what would be done when
Benny grew up and had long legs ;—would he still
go on sleeping there, with his legs dangling over the
end, or would mother buy him a new bed ? He often
wondered how this would be.

Froggy had many times prepared Benny's food in

the little pannikin, but he had never fed him and put
him to bed before, because mother had always done
that; but he managed it very nicely. Seated on a
low stool, with a grave frown on his brow, as if he
were fully alive to the responsibilities of handling so
tiny a scrap of humanity, first he fed his brother,
next undressed him, and put on his little night-shirt,
which was not much larger than a pocket-handkerchief, and then hushed him to rest (as he had seen
mother do) on the top of the Punch and Judy box.
He took care to tuck the clothing well in all round
under the mattress, so that Benny could not possibly
fall out during the night. After he had done all this,
he approached his father very softly, and said—

"Fader, dear! I've put Benny to bed: what shall
I do now?"

"Go to bed yourself, and be a good boy, and hold
your tongue," said his father in a whisper; and Froggy
without a word quietly retired to a corner, where there
was another little mattress spread on the floor, and
began undressing himself.

Froggy was very hungry, and would have liked
some supper, but he never said so. He felt that this
was no time for expressing any of his own wants with
poor mother lying there so still and so pale; and
father looking so grave. He must be quiet, as father
told him, and go to bed, and forget his hunger if he
could, in the face of the grievous trouble which
Froggy felt had somehow fallen upon them. He lay
down on his mattress and tried to sleep, but his eyes

stayed wide open, and he grew hungrier and hungrier. It was a strange scene that the poor little boy looked out upon ;—the miserable garret, with its bare damp walls, lit by a solitary tallow candle, whose flickering rays were trying hard to assert themselves in the current of air which blew from the window patched up with brown paper; the Punch and Judy show looming grimly opposite to him, in the corner where it was stabled for the night; little Benny lying asleep on the box; and, finally, the mattress on which Froggy's eyes were riveted, where his mother lay, and beside which his father sat, trying to feed her with some hot tea. He saw her take a few sips, and then, after a very long time, Froggy's eyes became drowsy, the lids dropped, and he fell asleep.

It must have been far into the night, nearly morning, when he awoke again. His father was still watching by the mattress, and he heard his mother's voice speaking.

"'Arry, dear," she said faintly, "I don't think I shall ever go out with the Punch again !"

Froggy thought he heard some sobs, but he was not sure.

"You've bin a good wife to me, Jeanie. You've borne with me kind ; and God knows I'm sorry for any unkind words I've spoke to you," said the husband after a moment ; and now Froggy was sure of the sobs, and he felt inclined to sob too.

Presently his mother spoke again.

"You must cheer up, 'Arry, and take care o' the

little uns. Send Froggy to night-school, and
Benny,"—her voice faltered here just a little,—
" when he's growed up, and tell 'em of the land where
I'm going."

At these words Froggy threw off the clothing that
covered him, and swift as a little hare darting from
its form, he ran across the floor with bare feet, and
stood by his mother's bedside.

"Mudder! mudder, dear! are you going to a new
land?" he cried with excitement. "Tell me about
it. What did I hear you say about going to a land?"

He waited for a moment with wide-opened, earnest
eyes fixed upon his mother's face, then getting no
answer, he turned and appealed to his father.

"Fader, dear! tell me, where is the land where
Mudder's going?" he pleaded almost passionately,
pulling at the poor man's hands that were covering
his face.

"Is it far to go? Does it take much money?
Where is it, Fader?"

"It's the Better Land, Froggy," sobbed the father,
" where everybody is happy."

"Then I'll go," cried Froggy. "O Mudder! where-
ever *you* go, me must go—Benny and me! And if it's
happier *there* than it is here, why don't we *all* go?"
he asked, looking from one to the other, as if the
wisdom of the proposition were unanswerable.

"Yes! all must come by and by," murmured
the mother softly. " Blessed Jesus! bring them all
home—'Arry, and Froggy, and Benny!" and then,

"Mudder! Mudder, dear! are you going to a new land?" he cried with excitement.

with a little sigh and the faintest sob, the mother's soul passed over to the eternal shores.

"Jeanie! Jeanie!" called the father in imploring accents; but there was no response. He uttered the exceeding bitter cry which so often goes up before God from the first agony of the bereaved soul.

"Oh, she's gone!" he sobbed aloud.

"Is Mudder in the Better Land now?" asked Froggy softly, looking up into his father's face.

"Yes, Froggy, she's there," he said, gazing blankly down upon him; "and she'll never be unhappy again, or footsore, or weary."

"Then that's good!" said Froggy. "Good-night, Fader, dear! I'm going back to my little bed again;" and he crept back and laid himself down.

For a long while after, he could hear his father sobbing beside his dead mother, and little Froggy turned his face to the wall and cried too, but he seemed to take peculiar comfort to himself in the thought that mother would never be footsore or weary again.

CHAPTER II.

THE RETURN FROM EPSOM.

FTER this night came some very sorrowful days, in which everything seemed strange and new to Froggy. The mother was buried, and they all followed her to the grave. In times of trouble, women, as a rule, come out bravely and well; and so the women did on this occasion. When it became known in the house that the Punch and Judy man upstairs had lost his wife, offers of kindly assistance came from more than one quarter; and the lodger below, who had little children of her own, mounted to the garret on the morning of the funeral, and tied some crape round the father's hat, and some upon Froggy's, and prepared to follow with them herself to the cemetery, with little Benny in her arms. And when they came back, she lit a fire for them, and cooked their dinner, and did all that she could to console and to help them during the rest of the day.

The next day, after the funeral, the father rose up early, and went out with the Punch and Judy show as usual. It does not do for the bread-winner to suspend work, even though he has lost his wife; and this poor man went about the squares and terraces at the West End, beating the drum, and " Oyoying!" up at all the windows, just as if nothing had happened, and there was no bitter grief at his heart. Froggy went with him, and took his mother's place by the side of the green curtain to keep off any little inquisitive boys who came too close. Not that Froggy could have done much, I think, if they had insisted upon having a peep, because he would have been too small to prevent them; but he held his head high, and looked as big as he possibly could for the occasion. Little Benny was left at home. Mrs Ragbon, the landlady, in a neighbourly spirit had told the father that, if he liked to leave him behind along with her own little brats of a day, and pay for his food, while he went Punch and Judying, she wouldn't so much mind. And the bereaved father, who could not afford to be too particular in his choice of a guardian for Benny, now that his mother was gone, thanked Mrs Ragbon, and left him with her gladly, notwithstanding that it was whispered amongst the other lodgers that, when the landlady had taken too much to drink, "she thumped her own brats about awful!"

Froggy in these days often had a sore cry to.himself, with a longing to see mother, and to kiss her. He did not wish mother back, but he wished he could go to mother. He never said so though, because he noticed that whenever he spoke of "Mudder," father turned away and sobbed, and it distressed Froggy beyond everything to see his father cry. He was very kind to his little brother, and if he got anything nice out with father during the day, such as a cake or an orange, he would be sure to bring half of it home to Benny at night. If he thought anybody had hurt Benny, or had not been kind to him in any matter, Froggy was very wrathful, and would plead for and protect him with all his might. It was good to see how he loved him, since he was shortly to become Benny's sole earthly protector in this great seething world, where everybody is struggling and fighting for his own, and the weak have often in worldly matters to go to the wall, unless they have some sturdy one to protect and care for them.

After mother's death, Froggy noticed a great change in father. He began to brush himself up on Sunday mornings, and to lead his little boy to the free seats of a neighbouring church, which Froggy used to think the most wonderful and beautiful place the world had ever seen. And well he might; for Froggy's standard of comparison for everything was the poor garret at Shoreditch! The grand sounds of the organ and the voices singing he always associated with his ideas of the Better Land where mother had gone. He remembered she used to speak of the angels, and the golden harps, and the songs of praise in heaven, and he thought that surely this must be something like it. And in the evenings, father would take out mother's Bible sometimes, and spell out to them stories—*such* beautiful stories—of Jesus of Nazareth, and His wonderful words of gentle love and kindness, about the lilies of the field, and His care of the little sparrows, which always seemed to touch and comfort Froggy's heart more than anything else!

As they trudged along their weary way day by day, Froggy noticed, too, that father often stopped at the beautiful drinking-fountains, where fresh, clear water flows all day for thirsty wayfarers, and not only drank deeply of it himself, but gave Froggy many a pleasant long draught out of the common cup. Towards evening once, on a hot summer's day, father halted at one of these fountains. Father was very warm and tired, and looked just as Froggy had often seen him look when he used to say he *must* go into a public-house for a drop of something, or he'd never have the strength to carry the Punch home. A favourite resort of his on these occasions had always been the " Red Lion," the glaring signboard of which shone out in red and gold close to where he and Froggy were standing now.

" There's the Red Lion, father, dear," said Froggy, looking up wistfully into his face. The man looked up at the house, and then sighed heavily. " You are not going in to-night for your drop o' drink, are you, father ? " said Froggy timidly.

" No, my boy; *this* is the best drink," he said, pointing to the fountain. " It cures the thirst, and keeps the head clear instead o' muddling it. I shall never go in there again, Froggy ! "

"*Never*, father?" said Froggy wonderingly; "why not?"

"Because I've taken the pledge, Froggy; and, by God's help, I'll never taste strong drink again."

Froggy marvelled what this wonderful thing could be,—the *pledge!* He had often heard his dead mother pleading with his father, even with tears in her eyes, to take it. He had never done so during her lifetime, that Froggy knew, for at their very last poor breakfast together he had heard her speak of it again. And *now*, father had taken it! He wondered whether dear mother knew: how pleased she would be if she did! Ah! yes, the pledge! what a blessed thing it is! How often Froggy's garret home was cheered now by father's loving ways and kindly care. It was frequently fragrant with the smell of hot coffee, and there were rashers of bacon occasionally on the grid-iron (which made little Benny rub his hands joyously when he smelt it frizzling over the fire), which would certainly never have been there if father had not left off spending his money at the gin-shops. In these days of improvement, father sent Froggy to a night-school, which had been established in Shoreditch. It was a very large one, and there were boys of all kinds and sizes there, and some grown-up men as well. Some amongst them had been thieves, I am afraid; but everybody found a welcome at the night-school, whatever they were, and no one was turned out as long as they behaved themselves properly and tried to learn. But there was always a policeman on duty

outside, ready to rush in and remove anybody who
was riotous or otherwise misbehaving himself. Sometimes there were shameful scenes at this night-school.
Wicked men and boys occasionally joined together,
and came in for the express purpose of making a dis-
turbance; they would whistle and laugh, and openly
defy the clergyman and the gentlemen who were
helping him, and it was with great difficulty that order
was restored. But these scenes were happily not fre-
quent. Froggy liked going to the night-school very
much, and he learnt to read and to write. He went
regularly twice a week till he was about eleven years
old and Benny was six; then something occurred
that I am going to tell you about, which prevented
Froggy from going any more.

It was one evening in May, in the height of what
the fashionable West End people call the London
season. Froggy and his father were returning from
Epsom after the great race of the Derby had been
run with their Punch and Judy show, which had
amused many a group of holiday folk on the breezy
Downs during the day. Though Froggy was tired,
and longing to be at home in the garret at Shoreditch
with Benny, he was very happy, because his father
had done a good day's business, and had given him
sevenpence for himself. After having had a good,
long lift with a friendly drayman, who was returning
with emptied beer-barrels from the race-course, they
had taken to their feet again, and were toiling along
a crowded thoroughfare, amidst a mighty stream of

pedestrians, cabs, carts, and omnibuses, when suddenly a shout was heard, and a four-in-hand drag, crowded with men in light coats and hats, with blue veils twisted round them, who were evidently more merry than wise, came rattling sharply round the corner. Everything, pedestrians, cabs, carts, and omnibuses, all pulled up, and got out of the way, except one poor man and his little boy! This was Froggy and his father. Froggy remembered hearing a woman scream loudly, then saw the Punch and Judy show knocked down, then felt himself knocked down violently too—had a dim recollection of a policeman hovering over him—lastly, a dream-like feeling of being floated along somehow and somewhere, he did not know whither, with all London surging and murmuring around him—and then nothing more till he woke up, and found himself—where? Not in the crowded roadway returning home with father and the Punch and Judy show from Epsom, but lying in a bed in a strange, clean place, with a screen round him, and a gentle-looking woman in a white cap standing by.

"Where am I?" asked Froggy, opening his eyes wide and staring.

"You are in a hospital, my boy. You've been hurt, but you are better now," said the gentle-faced woman kindly.

"Who brought me here?" asked Froggy.

"The police," said the nurse.

"When did I come?"

"Yesterday evening," she answered.

"Who are you, please?"

"I am the hospital nurse taking care of you."

"Thank you!" said Froggy, and then he did not speak again for a few moments. Suddenly he started up in bed as a tide of recollection swept over his brain, and he asked anxiously—

"Please, ma'am, where is father?"

"He was brought to the hospital yesterday at the same time as you were, my boy," said the nurse, taking Froggy's hand in hers. "He was in terrible pain, but I think he is quite happy now."

"Then he's not much hurt—he's gone home to Benny?" said Froggy eagerly.

"Who is Benny?" she asked.

"My little brother at Shoreditch," said Froggy.

The nurse came closer to him, and said, very kindly and gently, "No, that isn't the home where father's gone to. There is a beautiful home in the skies, my boy, where Jesus lives. Have you ever heard of it?"

"Yes," said Froggy; "it's called the Better Land, where mother went when she left Benny and me and father, a long while ago."

"Yes," said the nurse softly, "that is it; and that is where the good angels carried poor father yesterday when he was in that terrible pain."

"Won't he come back no more?" asked Froggy, looking at her with his pitiful eyes.

"No; but you will go to him," said the nurse comfortingly. "This is a sad world, and Jesus

thought it was time to take father out of it, and make
him happy."

"Then that is good!" murmured Froggy softly,
not able to realise at first that he would never see
his father again in this world.

" Ah ! my boy," said the nurse earnestly, "*always*
say that. Whatever Jesus sends you, try to say, 'That
is good;' whatever He takes away from you, try to
say, 'That is good;' and then, as long as you have
breath in your body, Jesus will *never* leave you."

" Not never till I die ? " said Froggy.

" Never ! never ! " said the nurse with the warmth
of one who has tried and proved for herself the
abiding love of Jesus.

" I must get up now, and go to Benny," said
Froggy, with a great look of care coming into his face,
that was painful to see in a child. " P'r'aps he's bin
alone ever since yesterday, and maybe he's not got
nothink to eat."

" You must wait till the doctor has been round
first," said the nurse; "he won't be long now. Ah!
here he comes ;" and as she spoke a small, grave-
looking gentleman approached the bedside, and began asking Froggy questions about himself.

" I feels quite well, sir," said Froggy, when he had
finished answering them ; "and I wants to go home
partiklar."

"Well, I think you may, my little man," said the
Doctor; "for you seem all right this morning."

" Please, I should like to see father once afore I

goes," said Froggy with big tears in his eyes, looking up pleadingly at the nurse and doctor, who exchanged glances at the question, and shook their heads. " I know he's in the Better Land, and never can't speak to me no more; but I'm thinking as how I'd just like to see his face once again, and touch his hand, as I did mother's when she was gone;" and now the little heart seemed wellnigh bursting with the first keen pang of the orphan's loneliness, and he sobbed aloud, wailing bitterly for some minutes.

The nurse covered her eyes for a moment, for Froggy had made the tears start to them, and the doctor said very kindly but firmly—

" I cannot let you see your father, my little fellow. I am sorry to refuse you, but I have a very good reason for doing so indeed ;" and poor Froggy did not press his wish further, for there was something in the doctor's tone and manner which impressed him with great confidence, and made him undoubtful of the wisdom of his refusal, though he could not guess the reason for it.

The fact was, the poor Punch and Judy man had been knocked down in the road, and the wheels of the four-in-hand drag had passed over his body, and disfigured him frightfully, so that it was no sight for a little boy like Froggy to gaze upon. It would probably have unnerved him, and greatly shocked him, which the doctor knew well enough, and this was why he refused Froggy.

" Please, sir," said Froggy after a minute, " where's

the Punch and Judy what belonged to we ? cos I'd
like to take it.   I'd put a chair inside it till I
growed, and show it off that way for Benny and
me."

"I hear it was smashed to pieces in the accident,
my boy," said the doctor.

Poor Froggy ! his heart sank at this.   Without
the friendly old Punch and Judy, which had kept
the wolf from the door and fire in the grate all
these years, what was to be done ?   How was he to
get food for Benny ?   This was the question that
had begun to trouble him from the very first
moment he knew his father was dead.   How was
he to get food for Benny ?   Poor brother Benny !
whose small, white face, crumpled up into a little
comical smile, was so perpetually before him, and
of which Froggy could hardly think without crying
when he imagined Benny hungry, or hurt, or
unhappy !

As he trudged along home after leaving the
hospital, with the money which had been found
in poor father's pockets, and which he calculated
was just enough to pay Mrs Ragbon the rent which
was owing to her, Froggy pondered much and
anxiously over that question, which is daily exer-
cising the brains of thousands in our great over-
grown city of London, how to get bread and work
to live ?   He must take to something which did
not require much outlay in the beginning, for
Froggy had only one and sevenpence ·in the world

to call his own—a shilling the doctor had presented
him with before leaving the hospital, and that sevenpence poor father had given him yesterday on
Epsom Downs. When he met a costermonger,
Froggy thought he would like to be one, to sell
vegetables and fruit; but then there was the barrow
to buy, and the stock, and he could not afford that.
Then he thought he would like to be a shoeblack,
but then he did not know what steps to take to
get into the Brigade, and he had no friends to help
him.

"No friends!" some of my readers will exclaim;
"why, where were his teachers at the night-school?"
Alas! Froggy's night-school was no more. A few
weeks ago, a great railway company, wanting more
land to build warehouses upon, had begun clearing
away whole streets of houses in the Shoreditch
neighbourhood, and, amongst the rest, the night-
school had been pulled down, and was not yet
re-opened in another place. Froggy, who did not
know where any of the teachers lived, but had
some vague idea of their being always at the night-
school, because he always saw them there when *he*
was there, never thought of seeking them out else-
where. If he had known the address of one of
these teachers, and had applied for it, he would soon
have got kindly help and advice in his difficulties.
Froggy's ideas had to come down much lower.
How would it do to sell cigar-lights or *Echoes*, or
to buy a broom and sweep a crossing? Ah! this

was the best thing, thought Froggy. A broom would not cost much, and he would choose some crowded thoroughfare, where there were plenty of foot-passengers, and make a good thing of it perhaps.

Having chosen his trade, Froggy felt relieved, and the poor little boy turned into a shop and bought a penny meat-pie to carry home to Benny, in case Mrs Ragbon had been drinking and allowed him to go hungry. And this was not an unlikely thing to have happened; for Mrs Ragbon, I am sorry to say, during these later years had taken much more freely to drink, in consequence of which her husband had deserted her, and her temper had become very violent and bad. She let everything go, and take its chance. She neglected even her own children, and therefore it was not to be expected that she would take any particular care of Benny, who was not her child, and had no particular claim upon her.

When Froggy reached the dismal house in Shoreditch, the landlady met him with very scowling looks.

"Where have you been to?" she asked in harsh tones; "where's your father?"

Froggy then in a broken voice, with many tears, told her of the accident coming from Epsom, and that father was dead.

"Dead!" repeated Mrs Ragbon looking aghast. "*Never!* and he alive and well the day before yesterday, and starting so cheery like for Epsom! Lor!

if that ain't awful!" she said, throwing up her hands.

"But I got the rent for you," said poor Froggy quickly, giving her the money.

"Well, that's a good thing; I can't afford to lose any o' that," she said roughly. "What do you intend to do with yoursels?"

"I means to sweep a crossing," said Froggy, with his cheeks getting a little red.

"Very well. Now listen to what I'm going to say," said the landlady severely, with her finger up, and shaking it at Froggy. "As long as you pays me fourpence a week reg'lar for the room up top, you may stay there, but the first Saturday as comes and you don't, I'll thrash you both, and turn you out o' doors, as I did my son Mac—recollect that, you young rascal!"

Mrs Ragbon called every little boy a rascal whom she met.

Seeing by Froggy's frightened face that he was duly impressed with the necessity of working to avoid the fate of Mac, she let him go, and Froggy ran up the steep stairs to Benny. He was playing with a little tame mouse, that used to come out of a hole in the garret and feed on the crumbs.

"I thought you was never coming home, Froggy," said Benny, jumping up from the floor, and leaving the mouse. "I feels so empty, I does!"

"Here's a nice pie," said Froggy; and his little brother snatched at it eagerly, having only had some crusts of bread that a friendly lodger, Mrs Blunt, had given him, since yesterday at one o'clock.

Benny's little face (which was rather a pitiful one, with a sort of "lost-half-a-crown-and-found-a-penny" look upon it), brightened marvellously at the sight of the meat-pie, and the rapidity with which he demolished it was astonishing.

"Shouldn't I like another!" said Benny with warmth when he had finished it. "Froggy, darlin! where's Fader?"

"He's gone to mother," said Froggy, putting his arm round Benny and clinging to him.

"Up in the sky where the stars twinkle?" asked Benny wonderingly.

"Yes, where God lives and the angels," said Froggy.

"And gentle Jesus, that I says my hymn to?" asked Benny.

"Yes," nodded Froggy; and then he told Benny all about the accident yesterday, and how poor father had been killed.

"Then we're all alone now, us two little men!" said Benny, looking very gravely up into Froggy's face. "Only I got you, and you got me. O Froggy! won't father never, *never* come back to take care of us no more? What *shall* we do? O Froggy, Froggy!" and the two little boys clung together and sobbed piteously for some minutes.

"No, we've got no one what'll take care of us now," said Froggy at last. "Mother's gone and father's gone, and we've not got no friends!"

What a sad reflection—motherless, fatherless, and friendless! But so it was; and this is the condition of hundreds of our poor little brothers and sisters in great London. Let us think of this next Sunday when the petition comes in our beautiful Litany, "That it may please Thee to defend and provide for the fatherless children and widows, and all that are desolate and oppressed!" and say from our hearts on their behalf, "We beseech Thee to hear us, good Lord!"

The owners of the drag, which had caused the death of Froggy's father, called at the hospital the next day to make what reparation they could for the accident which their reckless driving had brought about. But alas! too late. They were greatly dismayed to learn that their drunken carelessness had cost the life of a fellow-creature, and that the orphan boy had returned to his desolate home, without leaving any trace behind him.

CHAPTER III.

FROGGY AS BREAD-WINNER.

THE next morning Froggy was up betimes. He ran out, and got two penny-rolls from the nearest baker's for himself and Benny, and with a mug of water they breakfasted. Benny let some crumbs down on purpose for his pet, and by and by out came the little brown mouse from his hole, and cautiously approaching, with eyes very bright, came and nibbled industriously till they were all gone, and then retired quietly again without a sound. Benny did love his little mouse so! I do not know what he would have done if it had forsaken the garret. After this, Benny crept downstairs to seek with other children that which is a necessity of childhood—play; and poor Froggy, with all the cares of a bread-winner upon him, sallied forth into the busy streets to buy his broom and begin life as a crossing-sweeper. Before starting, he gave Benny twopence out of his little store, and told him to ask Mrs Blunt, the lodger underneath, to get him some dinner.

When he had bought his broom, Froggy began

looking about him with a keen eye to business for a
suitable crossing. He settled that it must be one
where there was plenty of traffic, and in a shopping
neighbourhood, so that people coming from shops
would be likely to have coppers in change to throw to
him. This was not such an easy thing to get as he
had imagined, and Froggy found himself a long way
from home before he found the kind of crossing he
wanted unoccupied. At last, however, he halted, and
took up his position at a point where four roads met
in a crowded thoroughfare, close to a station of the
Metropolitan Railway. An old woman with a
cherry-stall, seated serenely under an umbrella to
keep off the sun, with her feet in a basket, knitting
a grey stocking, had planted herself as usual for the
day at this busy point, and also a little shoeblack
boy, who it appeared was in no way dependent on
dirty streets for employment, as he was busy with
his blacking-pot and brushes already, though it
was so fine. Froggy wished the weather had been wet
and bad, for it would have given him a better chance
at his crossing, which was really so clean as to require
no sweeping at all. But still Froggy swept, notwithstanding the little shoeblack boy called out chaffingly,
" I ses, matey, you'll make your fortun at that, I can
see ! " and other boys chaffed him as well. But
Froggy did not mind the chaff. Whatever work
bread depends upon is such a serious matter, we
cannot easily be laughed out of it ; and Froggy was
ever mindful that little Benny's bread depended upon

his efforts at this crossing. He did not take a penny
for a long time. The road became very crowded as
the day wore on, and people passed and repassed by
hundreds, all so intent upon their own business that
no one seemed to cast a thought upon him. The
old woman sold her cherries, and the shoeblack boy
was continually on his knees polishing boots;—
everybody seemed to be getting in their money but
himself. He thought he would compel people to
notice him somehow, and with a view to this he took
to running in front of foot-passengers, looking up into
their faces, and saying, "Please, sir, throw us a copper!"
"Please, 'm, 'member the sweeper!" One gentleman
said, "Certainly not! what do we want sweepers for
in this fine weather?" and passed on. Yes! but did
the gentleman remember that poor little sweepers
want bread to eat in *fine* weather as well as in bad?
One lady said, "Oh, get along, you little bore! you
as nearly as possible tripped me up;" but she threw
him a penny nevertheless. Oh, how pleased Froggy
was! How he dived in between the cabs and omnibuses to look for it, for it had rolled, and he could not
see it at first. The shoeblack boy, who had chaffed
him earlier in the day, now did him a good turn,
and called out, "I sees it, matey; there it be, nigh to
the kerb!" and following the direction of his hand,
Froggy soon spied it out, and pocketed it.

It was now twelve o'clock, and everybody seemed
to be having their luncheon or dinner. Froggy saw
a little girl bring something in a yellow basin tied up

in a speckled handkerchief to the old woman at the
cherry-stall, and watching with interested eyes, he
soon decided to his satisfaction that it was hot beefsteak pudding.' Presently the shoeblack boy produced
a handkerchief and a clasp-knife from his pocket, and
began eating a huge sandwich of bread and meat.
Numerous people darted into a neighbouring pastry-
cook's about this time, and darted out again shortly
after with their teeth buried in a hot bun or crunch-
ing a captain's biscuit. Everybody, indeed, appeared
to be eating. Froggy was getting very hungry, and
every now and then looked longingly at the pastry-
cook's, where there were so many nice things to be
got for a penny, but he could not make up his mind
to part with the one he had till he had earned
another. By and by an opportunity occurred. A
Metropolitan train was just in, and a crowd of passengers, as usual, came swarming up the steps into
the street. Some marched briskly off at once, some
called cabs, some hailed omnibuses, and others
stopped and had their boots polished by the little
shoeblack who called Froggy "matey." Amongst
the passengers whom the train disgorged on this
occasion was a very stout red-faced old woman, with
bonnet-strings untied and gloves off, who bore the
appearance of having gone through some very violent
struggle underground. She was panting and blowing
asthmatically, and notwithstanding a bunch of flowers,
a large gingham umbrella, and a bag in one hand, she
was trying to fan herself with the other by means of a

c

pocket-handkerchief, which she had twisted somehow
into a hard ball like the top of a drumstick—a very
inefficient fan one would think, but it seemed nevertheless to be affording her relief.

This poor old woman, I must tell you, had been to
Sydenham to see a friend, and the weather being very
warm, and herself very stout, and not being an expert
traveller on this line of railway, she came to the top
very much out of breath, and feeling, as I have said
she looked, as though she had gone through a most
exhausting struggle.   What with getting into the
wrong carriages, losing her ticket, missing trains, and
battling with the officials, &c., &c., she may fairly be
said to have gone through something !

After a moment or two, recovering her breath, she
seemed to brace herself up again for another tussle,
and advancing to the edge of the pavement with a
determined air, began watching her opportunity to
cross.   Several times did she leave the pavement; each
time did she have to trundle back, for either a cab was
coming or an omnibus was coming, or a something
which threatened danger if she persisted.   After
her fifth endeavour, which proved as unsuccessful as
the other four, she became very irate and highly
indignant.

" Where *is* the p'leece ? " she cried out at last quite
loud, and looking about her in all directions for that
much-abused body.   "It's a positive scandal how they
never is to be found when they're wanted.   If Colonel
Fraser or Colonel 'Enderson, or whoever he is as

commands the p'leece, would only come by at this moment, I'd give him such a talking-to as never he had in his life before !" and she looked so extremely vindictive, that I think the Chief Commissioner would certainly have repented it if circumstances had brought him into her neighbourhood at this moment.

Giving the pavement an angry rap with the end of her gingham, she was just on the point of holding forth again, when she heard a little boy's voice close to her, saying, "Please, 'm, do you wants to cross t'other side ?" and looking down, she saw Froggy with his broom staring very anxiously up into her face.

"Wants to cross! o' course I do," replied the old woman, glad to have even a little crossing-sweeper to listen to her. "Here I've been to Sydenham, and comes back early, though sister-law begged me to stay tea and go to the Palice, purpose to avoid all noosances, and to get 'ome comfortable, and here I'm kept at this crossing ten minutes by the clock, and not a p'leeceman to be seen to take me over! It's a scandal !"

"Here," thought Froggy, "is a fine opportunity."

"I'll take you, mum," said he ; "let *me*, mum."

"Could you ? would you ? do you think you could now?" said the old woman, becoming quite affable at the prospect of help. "I'll give you a silver three-penny if you will."

"Ketch hold o' me, mum, and *I'll* take you as safe as safe !" said Froggy confidently.

No need to tell her to "ketch hold!" Laying a heavy hand on Froggy's shoulder, she clutched at it with a grip of iron, as if her very life depended on clinging to him, though his little rough head barely reached her elbow.

"Wait a bit, mum; don't get flustered," said Froggy, feeling it was no light frigate he had in tow. "Let them two cabs pass, and that 'bus, and then—— *Now*, mum, step out!" and off they started on the perilous journey across. Midway Froggy pulled up. "Stop a bit, mum," he said; "'ere's a 'bus coming."

For a moment the old woman became completely frenzied. Turning her head and seeing the pole of the omnibus in the distance, she screamed as if it had already struck her, and in her agitation she dropped her gingham and her oilskin bag, which was bulging with Sydenham carrots and cabbages, and out they rolled all over the road.

"Never mind, mum; *I'll* pick 'em up," called out Froggy in a high tone of encouragement.

"Never mind the carrots, boy; get me over, that's all I cares for!" shrieked the old woman loudly; but she altered her tone somewhat when, a minute later, Froggy landed her safely on the opposite side.

"Me carrots! me cabbages! and me bag! Lor! boy, try and save 'em," she cried.

The little crossing-sweeper needed no urging; without a moment's hesitation he darted in gallantly amongst the cabs and omnibuses, as he had done for his own penny, and began picking up the scattered

"In her agitation she dropped her gingham and her bag, which was bulging
with carrots and cabbages, and out they rolled all over the road."

Page 36.

vegetables right and left. The old woman stood on the pavement cheering him on, and almost waving her gingham in her excitement.

"Capital, me boy!" she exclaimed; "well done! good, good!" as she saw him rescue a cabbage from an imminent cab-wheel. "Excellent! well done!" And when at last Froggy returned to her with his arms full of carrots right up to his chin, and with her bag and cabbages as well, she dived into her pocket, and brought out her purse, saying, "You're a first-rate boy!" and gave him, not a threepenny-piece, but a shilling; and not only a shilling, but one of the nice Sydenham carrots, which she informed him would "eat very well raw."

Oh! for Froggy's delight over this shilling and this carrot. The shilling would pay for a whole week's rent, and for some food besides; and the carrot—what a nice supper he and Benny would have to-night! The carrot cut in half would be plenty for both, and with a penny meat-pie each, and some bread, which Froggy could now buy, they would have a supper fit for a king. Of course Froggy got something to eat after this, but his refreshment was a very moderate one in view of the sumptuous supper he and Benny were to have.

The day wore on, and at seven o'clock the old woman packed up her cherry-stall, and went home for the night. The shoeblack boy did the same with his box, and Froggy thought it was time for him to go home too. So he shouldered his broom and marched briskly homewards, only stopping on his way to buy the two meat-pies and the loaf of bread for supper. Thus ended Froggy's first day as a crossing-sweeper.

CHAPTER IV.

SUPPERLESS.

TOWARDS nine o'clock on this long summer's evening, just when it was beginning to get dark in the garret at Shoreditch, the two little brothers, Froggy and Benny, were sitting huddled up together on the window-sill, enjoying their evening repast. Their knees were touching to make a table, and they had a handkerchief spread between them by way of tablecloth, on which they had their meat-pies, their bread, and the carrot. Over the latter they seemed to have gone into partnership, for they were taking a bite by turns, just in the same way as they were sharing a mug of water. Poor little fellows! how they were munching away and enjoying themselves!—Froggy like a grave old man, and Benny looking like a queer little Irish beggar in a tiny suit of corduroy (which had been Froggy's once), with his hair all over his eyes, and his little bare feet dangling below the articles he called his trousers. "Froggy, when I was playin in the street to-day, I saw *Mac*," said Benny, as if it were a grand piece of news.

Mac was the eldest son of the landlady, and had been turned out of doors by his mother because he would not work.   Some said he was a wicked boy, and deserved it; others said he had been treated harshly, and were inclined to cry "shame" on Mrs Ragbon for having cast him adrift.   Mac was an object of the intensest interest to both Froggy and Benny, who had often played with him; and anything they could learn of his movements, now that he was cast on the streets without a home, they gathered in with the keenest relish.

"Did you?" said Froggy eagerly.   "What was ee doing?"

"Walkin down the street like any other man!" said Benny.

Mac was only two years older than Froggy, and therefore not a *man* at all, but Benny called every little boy "a man."

"How was he dressed?" asked Froggy.

"Well, he had a nice little coat on," said Benny, "but his trousers was torn, and I could see his leg."

"Did he see you?" asked Froggy.

"Yes, cos I called out 'Hi, Mac!' and he came over and spoke to me," said Benny; "and Jack was with me, and he spoke to Jack too."

Jack was a playfellow of Benny's, though much older than Benny.

"What did Mac say?" inquired Froggy.

"He said he was very merry, and had lots o' grub and nice mates," replied Benny; "only sometimes the p'leece bothered him, and two times he has nearly bin took by the Board."

"The Board" meant the school-board officers, who were held in great terror by all the ragged street-urchins of the neighbourhood.

"Did he say anythink more?" asked Froggy.

"No, nothink more," said Benny, "'cept this. He put his thumb up to his nose at the house, and called out ever so loud, 'That's for my old mudder!' and then he ran away."

"That was wicked," said Froggy.

"Cos she couldn't catch him?" said Benny.

"No, cos it was rude to his mother—that's why," said Froggy. "The teacher as taught me at night-school said it was in the Bible never to say nothink rude to mother or father."

"Didn't Jesus ever say nothink rude to His mudder?" inquired little Benny.

"No, never," said Froggy.

"I wish I 'ad a mudder!" sighed Benny; "oh, I'd love her so! I'd never be rude to her, never! Look, Froggy, darlin! the little stars are 'ginning to come out;" and turning his eyes up from the dingy garret window to the blue eternities above, he began repeating the lines Froggy had taught him—

> "Twinkle, twinkle, little star!
> 'Ow I wonder what you are,
> Up above the world so high,
> Like a dimant in the sky!"

"Now, haven't we 'ad a supper *just?*" exclaimed

Froggy with satisfaction when everything was done, shaking the crumbs out on the floor, and folding up the handkerchief.

"Yes, and we not eaten too close neither," said Benny, jumping down from the window; "there's plenty for mouse. Ee's bin watchin us with his little hi ever so long. Yes, I's seen you, you dear bootiful little thing, you!" he called out in high glee as the mouse came running nimbly across the garret from under a chair to the spot where the crumbs lay scattered. "I wouldn't sell you for a shilling! I wouldn't sell you not to be the Prince o' Wales!" cried out Benny, going into ecstasies over his pet.

"It's time to go to bed now," said Froggy, giving himself a stretch; and the two little brothers knelt down and said their prayers. Froggy said his first, and got into bed; then little Benny followed with his.

"Pray, God, bless Froggy and me," he said, "and my little mouse, and take us and Deb to the Better Land when Froggy and me dies, where mudder went a long time ago, and now poor fadder's gone. For gentle Jesus' sake. Amen."

Then Benny crept quietly on to the mattress beside Froggy, the mouse ran back to his hole, and the garret was soon quite still.

"Froggy, are you asleep?" whispered Benny presently.

"No, not quite," answered the tired little breadwinner from under the clothes. "Say this thing and then don't talk no more."

"I was only thinking," said Benny, "how nice it would be, Froggy, if *every* day an old woman would want to cross, and us and mouse could 'ave a nice supper like this one to-night *always!*"

"Yes, it would be very nice," said Froggy sleepily. "Good-night! Don't speak no more."

"No," said Benny softly, and he lay very still, till, like Froggy, he fell asleep.

The next morning, and for many, many mornings long after, as regularly as clockwork, Froggy rose up early and went to his crossing. But by no means could he get shillings and carrots every day. Indeed, it was not long before poor little Froggy found out that crossing-sweeping was anything but a paying business. Sometimes there were old women and nervous ladies wanting to be conducted across the road, like the old woman of the first day, and of course Froggy was always ready and willing for the work, but he never fell in with one who was so liberal as to give him a shilling and a carrot again. Two-pence or threepence was the most they ever paid him for his services.

While the summer lasted, and the days were long, Froggy managed to earn enough to pay Mrs Ragbon her fourpence a week regularly for rent, and to keep himself and his little brother supplied with food. But when the days shortened, and the winter set in, these poor little boys entered upon some new and very bitter experiences.

The winter of '73—which is the one I am writing

about—will long be remembered by the poor of
London as being one of the hardest they have ever
known, because of the great strikes in the Welsh
coal-mines, which raised the price of coal to such an
extent, that some of the wealthiest houses in the land
began to economise their gas, and to knock off any
fires they were able to do without. When coal went
up in price, the other necessaries of life, meat and
bread, went up too, so that to thousands of poor souls
the struggle for bare existence became harder and
more terrible than ever. Many a poor hard-working
mother had the anguish of seeing the frail and deli-
cate one of the family quietly droop and fade out of
the world for the want of being properly warmed and
comforted. There were empty cradles where the
babies used to lie; there were empty chairs where the
old folks used to sit; and there was grief, none the less
deep because it was mute, in many a lowly kitchen
and garret in the suffering East End. They kept up
their spirits over it in a wonderful way, but the truth
was that poor little Froggy and Benny were nearly
starved with cold and hunger up in their miserable
garret. They were often miserably off for food ; and
as to fire, they never thought of such a thing, even on
the bitterest days, except when Benny and some
other half frost-bitten little boys and girls made a
pilgrimage to a rubbish heap in the neighbourhood,
where, if they were fortunate, they could sometimes
pick up sufficient wood and rubbish to kindle a fire
large enough to fry a herring by or to make a kettle

boil. But it was very seldom they had anything to cook. Dry bread and onions were what they chiefly existed upon, meat being a luxury seldom dreamed off in these days.

When there was nothing to eat, Froggy and Benny never despaired ; they bore their poverty and misery like little heroes. Froggy seemed only miserable about it because of Benny, and Benny seemed mostly to care because of Froggy and his mouse. If " mouse " had no crumbs to eat, he took it greatly to heart, and had lately added this petition to his prayers—" Pray, God, make my little mouse stop in his hole. Don't let 'im think he'll go somewhere else. Please, God, tell 'im the winter will soon be over, and Froggy ses better days is coming!" It was Benny's greatest fear that the mouse would desert its hole.

One miserable December evening, after having been at his crossing all day in the snow and cold, poor Froggy was returning home without even having taken as much as a halfpenny! The weather had been such, that not even the old woman with her apple-stall had come out, and she was generally there on the most hopeless days. The shoeblack boy had not been at his usual post either, and any passengers arriving by the Metropolitan trains, and coming out of the station, hailed a cab or an omnibus at once, and very few availed themselves of the neat crossing Froggy had swept in the snow. At any rate, no one paid him for it, and he shouldered his broom at six o'clock to go home without having taken, as I have said, even a single halfpenny.

I wonder whether my little Froggy was the boy of whom the writer was thinking when he wrote the following touching lines on a little crossing-sweeper for whom he could not find a copper. Likely enough!

> "'Twas nothing but a vulgar little chap,
> A dirty, ragged, red-nosed, hungry wight;
> And all he did was just to touch his cap,
> When, feeling in my pocket one cold night,
> I could not find the halfpenny I sought;
> And when he saw my search was all in vain,
> With gentle tone of gratitude for nought,
> Said, 'Thank you, sir!' and turned him round again.
> And then I heard him whistling: very slow
> And feeble first his tones, as though a chill
> Had damped his music with a tinge of woe;
> Yet but a while, and he commenced a trill
> Of some street composition's jerky air,
> That grew and grew, and louder rattled out,
> Until he danced as though he tried to wear
> His very feet, if not the pavement, out!
> Then with redoubled vigour all around
> He plied his besom with a frantic will,
> As if his tune had made his soul rebound;
> And when I left him, he was whistling still.
> I met him ne'er again, but always kept
> My pocket ready with a copper store;
> For since, in musings, and whene'er I slept,
> A ragged little figure oft I saw;
> And late that winter night in easy-chair,
> Whene'er the glowing embers chanced to stir,
> I seemed to see that young face aged with care,
> And hear that little voice say, 'Thank you, sir!'"

"I can't buy no bread now," thought Froggy as he

trudged along. "But we've got a supper, so we are not so bad off after all."

The *supper* Froggy was reckoning upon was a piece of good, wholesome Australian meat, which Mrs Ragbon in a fit of generosity had given him the day before, and of which there was still a small portion remaining when he had started out in the morning. The moment Froggy reached the garret, which was as cold as an ice-house, feebly lit by the end of a dismal tallow candle, he was met by Benny, with his hair very rough and tumbled, as if he had been rolling.

"Well, Froggy, 'ow much money 'as you got?" asked he, thrusting his little hands deep in his trousers-pockets, and looking very eager.

"Not a stiver!" said Froggy mournfully, throwing down his broom.

"A stiver! what's that?" asked Benny.

"It means nothink—not a farden!" exclaimed Froggy. "But it don't matter not so *very* much, you know, Benny, cos we've got that meat."

At the mention of the meat, a very comical look spread itself over Benny's face, and when Froggy moved towards the corner of the garret to fetch the meat from where he had left it in the morning standing on a box, Benny followed close behind with his shoulders shrugged up to his ears, as if he were trying to keep in some capital joke. To Froggy's astonishment, when he got to the box, he saw that the meat was gone! There was the plate,

but no meat—where could it be? Froggy stared
blankly at the empty plate for a minute, then
turned round upon Benny.

"I ses, Benny, the meat's gone!" he said,—"clean
gone! Whoever can a taken it? Do you know
anythink about it?" he asked searchingly, as he
caught a twinkle in Benny's eye.

"Yes; I saw it go," said Benny, evidently with
a strong inclination to laugh.

"Where did you see it go?" asked Froggy
quickly.

"Out at the door," said Benny.

"Who took it out at the door?"

"The cat!" said Benny; and then his little comical
face puckered up, his mouth went all to one side;
he gave a jump forward with his knees bent and
his shoulders up to his ears, and burst out into a
perfect peal of laughter, which, however, rather
abruptly ended, as he thought of Froggy's empty
pockets.

I must tell you that Benny was a rare little fellow
for laughing—indeed, quite irrepressible in this depart-
ment; and though he had lost his supper, and would
have to go to bed hungry, the idea of the cat having
taken it so amused him, he was unable to keep
quite grave over the fact when he had to record
it to Froggy.

"The *cat* took it! But how came you to let him?"
exclaimed Froggy, who was ravenously hungry, and
could not see the joke of it at all.

"I didn't let 'im," said Benny; "he never give me the chance o' saying 'No,'—he was so sly, and did it so quick."

"Where was you when he come?" asked Froggy.

"I was lyin down on the bed," said Benny, trying to look grave, but not succeeding, "cos I was feelin very empty; and I lit the candle, and set open the door, so as to hear when you come home, Froggy. And while I was lyin there very quiet," said Benny in a whisper, "I saw mister Tom Cat come creepin', creepin' round the door, and all at once he made a dart, like that, at the box"—(Benny darted forward to show Froggy)—"and he took the meat in his mouth, and ran off like mad, afore ever I could tell 'im to stop. *Won't* I give him a hit when I meets 'im next!" said Benny, with a nod of his head.

"Don't never hit 'im," said Froggy. "P'r'aps he was clemmed like we, and didn't know as how he was doing wrong."

"Oh, but I think he did," said Benny, screwing up one eye, and putting on a little knowing look. "Fact, I'm sure he did, Froggy; for ee came round the door so soft, and made a dart ever so quick at the meat, cos he was afraid of being caught."

"Well, I wish he had left us *half*," said poor Froggy; "he might a done that. We can't have no supper, Benny, to-night, cos there's no money to buy none."

"Never mind, Froggy, darlin!" said Benny. "It's

D

very bad, though, to be so hungry, that it is!   Let's
go to bed, Froggy, and cuddle together and get warm,
and we'll pretend we're not hungry.   It's very orkard
not having no money, Froggy, ain't it?" said poor
little Benny.

"Yes," said Froggy despondingly, "very orkard
indeed."

"I couldn't a done it, if I had bin the cat; could
you, Froggy?" said Benny pitifully.   "He feeds
better than we."

"Maybe he don't," said Froggy.

"Oh, but he do," replied Benny, "cos he gets all
the rats and mouses, and I sees 'im get nice little
bits of meat on sticks that the man sells in the streets,
that I should like to get a nip at."

"Well, I think *I* could eat a bit o' cat's meat to-
night," said poor Froggy.   "I'm that empty, I could
eat *anythink!*"

"A black beetle?" asked Benny.

"Don't be a silly!" answered Froggy; and then,
staring at Benny for a moment, he said suddenly—

"I ses, Benny, 'ow big your eyes is growing!"

Ah! poor little Benny!   It was not really that his
eyes were growing bigger, but that his face was growing thin.   It looked so small, and so white and sad,
it seemed to strike quite a pain into Froggy to-night,
and he clasped Benny tighter than ever in his arms
when they got on to the mattress and nestled together to keep warm.

'Froggy, do you think Mudder and Fader knows

we're hungry, in the Better Land?" asked Benny softly.

"No, cos it would make 'em fret like, and there's not nothink o' that sort in the Better Land," replied Froggy.

"I think I'd like to go there," said Benny with a little sigh.

"And leave me!" exclaimed Froggy, with a strange feeling of desolation coming over him lest some day he should be left all alone.

"Oh no, Froggy, darlin! I shouldn't like to go without you and Deb." (Deb was Benny's favourite playfellow, and lived in the room underneath.) "But I'd like to see Jesus, Froggy—wouldn't you? He was werry kind to little chaps like we, wasn't He, Froggy?"

"Yes, very," said Froggy.

"Maybe He'll take us afore we starve," murmured Benny half asleep. "Good night, Froggy, darlin!"

"Good night, Benny!" and they fell asleep after this, Benny sucking his fist as he used when he was a baby, and slept on the Punch and Judy box, and Froggy with a dark shadow over his face, as if in his dreams hunger and care were still pressing heavily upon him.

CHAPTER V.

MAC'S VISIT.

THE first thing Froggy saw, when he opened his eyes the next morning, was a little fluffy sparrow looking in at the window. It had a nice bit of bread in its mouth, and Froggy thought, " Oh, what a happy little sparrow! he's got *his* breakfast, and poor Benny and me's got none! "

As the bird flew away over the house-tops with the breakfast God had provided for it, some words came suddenly into Froggy's mind, which sounded as distinctly as if an angel's voice had whispered them, "Fear not! ye are of more value than many sparrows! "

" P'r'aps if I gets up, and looks about me like that there little sparrar, God'll send Benny and me a breakfast," thought Froggy. " I'll get up quick, and see if Mrs Blunt won't lend me twopence. She did it once afore, and I paid her again quite honest."

Froggy crept quietly out of bed, so as not to wake Benny, and went softly down the stairs. The landing below was rather dark, but Mrs Blunt's door was open, and through it the pale grey light came slanting

out from the window of her room. By it Froggy
could see that there was a burly man stooping over
a large tin can, from which he was dealing out milk
to the charwoman, who stood in the doorway. Froggy
heard Mrs Blunt say in a cheerful tone—

"Well, master, it ain't often we sees you. What's
the matter with Peggie that *you* comes to-day ?"

"Well, Peggie's had a haccident," replied the man.
"Slipped down on a piece of orange-peel, and given
her foot a nasty rick. But I wouldn't let you poor
folks go without your milk, thinkin o' the babies
and all; so master comes hisself you see. Why, whoever is this ?" he exclaimed, as the deplorable little
apparition óf Froggy came stealing down the stairs,
barefooted and large-eyed, and very miserable altogether.

"Why, its *Froggy !*" said Mrs Blunt. "Well,
Froggy," addressing him, "what brings you down this
time o' the morning, eh ?"

"Please, mum," said Froggy earnestly, "I come to
see if you'll lend me twopence, mum. Benny and
me's got no breakfast. We 'ad no supper last night
neither, and we're *awful* hungry this mornin'."

"Dear ! dear !" said Mrs Blunt sadly. "Oh yes,
Froggy, I'll lend it you ;" and she began fumbling in
her pockets.

"I'll pay it you back, mum, as sure as ever," said
Froggy gratefully.

"Oh yes, I'm not afraid o' that—I knows you're
honest," said Mrs Blunt, bringing out the coppers.

"'Ere they be then!" and she dropped them into Froggy's outstretched hand.

He thanked her (evidently from his heart), and was just turning off with the money, when the milkman, who had been standing by and listening, called out benevolently—

"Stop a bit, little shaver! Here! what should you say, I wonder, to a bowl of milk for breakfast? Should you like it?"

Froggy was quite unable to answer for a moment, but the charwoman answered for him.

"God bless you, master! It would be a Christian thing to do," she said. "Froggy, run up and get the master your jug—he's agoin to give you a breakfast."

The words now rang out in Froggy's heart quite loudly and triumphantly, "Fear not! ye are of more value than many sparrows!" and with a joy that was almost too much for him, he ran up into the garret, and fetched down the broken thing they dignified by the name of *jug*.

"Oh, sir, *sir!*" gasped Froggy at length, as he handed it to the milkman, and saw it plunged deep down into the depths of the milk-can. "Whatever can us do? Whatever can us say, Benny and me?"

"Why, just thank God for it, that's what'll be best," said the man cheerily, with a look of extreme satisfaction on his face, as he brought the jug out, and handed it back to Froggy all overflowing and dripping with the milk. "Now you only wants twopenn'orth o' bread to make a *real* good breakfast. If I stands the bread, missus, will you boil it all up for 'em, and make it hot ? " he asked, looking at Mrs Blunt.

"Yes, master, and glad I'll be to do it," she answered. "To be sure it's a hill wind that blows nobody any good! Now, if Peggie hadn't a hurt herself, Froggy, the master never would a come, and then you'd never have 'ad this fine breakfast."

"Was ever such a thing heard of?" thought Froggy,—"*hot bread and milk* for breakfast!" He was quite unable to express his thanks to the milk-man, but he *looked* them; and I am quite sure that that good man would have felt himself more than repaid for his generosity if he could have looked into the garret a quarter of an hour later. There was Froggy standing by the bedside holding aloft the beautiful basin of hot bread and milk, and little rough-headed hungry Benny sitting up with, oh, such eager eyes ! literally shouting for joy at the sight of it !

Froggy did not forget to thank God for the break-fast, as the milkman had told him to do. He knelt down presently, and said aloud for himself and Benny, "O God! Benny and me's *so* much obliged ! We've had such a beautiful breakfast ; it's warmed us so, and we feels quite comforted. It was the milkman that give it us, but we know, God, it come from you, cos you put it into his heart to be kind just as it's put into the hearts o' people to throw out crumbs for the little sparrars, so that they don't starve. Please, God, Benny and me's *very* much obliged !" and little Benny said heartily—

"Yes, please, God! Amen."

Then Froggy rose up from his knees, and went out to his crossing quite comforted.

One Sunday afternoon, about four o'clock, just when London was getting dark, and the lamps were being lighted in the gloomy streets, Froggy and Benny were busy over a handful of fire made up of odds and ends from the rubbish heap, trying to toast a herring for their tea. They called this meal *tea*, because it was the time when most people had it, but there was no real tea in the matter. Water was the only beverage these little boys knew, and instead of a teapot they had a jug of water, and instead of tea-cups, little mugs set out on a chair without a back to it, which served as a table, and on which there was also a broken plate, placed in readiness to receive the herring as soon as it was done. Froggie was on his knees holding the small fish close to the bars, at the end of a short fork, with his grave old man's face looking much interested over the cooking of it ; and crouching close by was Benny, with his rough head bent forward, and a pair of very eager eyes fixed on the herring, in which he was evidently as much interested as Froggy.

"I think he's getting done, Froggy," said Benny, meaning the fish, " cos ee's 'ginning to frizzle!"

"Well, it's a'most time," said Froggy. " He'll eat splendid, I know. I'll just give 'im a toasting t'other side, and then we'll enjoy 'im ever so much ! "

Froggy spoke with warmth, as if he were very

hungry, as indeed he was, and knew Benny to be the
same. There was a sharp frost outside, and the prospect of getting anything hot to eat was very grateful
to them.

"I wish we 'ad somethink nice to drink," said
Benny; " the water's so cold, it makes my little inside
have a pain. Don't you wish, Froggy, we 'ad some
beer ? "

" Beer ! " exclaimed Froggy. " No, I'd sooner have
some hot coffee, like what they sells at the stalls a
penny a cup. But whatever do you know about
beer?" he asked, because he could not remember when
Benny had ever tasted it.

"Oh, I often gets a little sip," replied Benny. "When
Jack goes for his mudder's beer, I meets him sometimes, and ee tips up the jug, and I gets quite a nice
little drink at it ! "

" You shouldn't never do that," said Froggy, looking severely at Benny. " That's what they calls in
the Catechism ' pickin' and stealin',' cos the beer
don't belong to you or to Jack ; and, 'sides that, it's
very bad for boys to drink beer. Mother always said
so when I was little, and said she hoped I'd never
drink it, never—not even when I was a man and
growed up—cos it was beer that made poor father
always poor, and kept us so short in the garret. I
thinks when I'm a man, I'll take the pledge; they says
it's capital for savin', and makin home comfortable ! "

How wise of Froggy ! If every boy and every
girl would make the same resolution to take the

pledge of temperance, and keep to it, what a good
thing it would be !   Those who go amongst the poor,
and have opportunities of studying London sorrow
and London sin, will invariably tell you that beer and
strong drink are at the bottom of it all.

"Froggy," said Benny, moving closer and speaking
confidentially, "shall I tell you somethink Jack has
told me?"

"Yes," said Froggy.

"Who do you think it's about?" asked Benny,
liking to keep Froggy expectant.

"I guess its about Mac," said Froggy.

"Yes it is," replied Benny ; and then lowering his
voice mysteriously, and speaking almost in a whisper,
he said—

"Well, Froggy, do you know Jack says Mac drinks
beer, and *he gets tipsy just like a man !* "

Benny looked at Froggy, and nodded his head to
confirm what he had just announced, for Froggy
looked as if he scarcely believed it.

"And somethink else too," added Benny; "he
smokes real bacca-pipes ! "

" He'll suffer for it some day," said Froggy, with the
air of an old man; "boys that does them sort o'
things always does.   That's p'r'aps why he's never
growed, and ain't so tall as me, though he's older."

"I nebber knew boys could get tipsy like men,
did you, Froggy?" asked Benny, looking up into
Froggy's face.

"No, I don't know as I did," said Froggy ponderingly ; then, as the herring began to frizzle furiously, he cried out, "Now then, Benny ! the dish ! the dish ! ee's done prime now ! "

And in another minute or two the little brothers were seated opposite each other, with the broken chair serving as table between them, devouring the hot herring and some dry crusts of bread with the eagerness and rapidity of half-famished beings.

It is terrible and painful to see hungry dogs taking to their food in this way, but thrice painful is it when we see hungry boys doing so. They had not proceeded far in their meal when they were startled by hearing a footstep coming cautiously and very quietly up the ricketty stairs outside. Visitors to the garret were so unfrequent, Froggy and Benny could not imagine who it could be coming up to see them. Mrs Ragbon came occasionally for her rent, but then she always mounted with a clatter, and the stairs were only creaking now under a very light weight. Froggy and Benny paused in their eating, and fixed their eyes steadily on the door, waiting to see who would enter.

"It may be only the cat ! " said Benny beneath his breath; but as he spoke the handle of the door turned softly, plainly showing it was not the cat, and in another minute a two-legged visitor entered. It was a ragged boy of stunted growth, with yellow hair, that looked as if it had never been combed or brushed for months, and with a red dissipated countenance, sadly suggestive of unlimited beer-

drinking and low companions. He was dressed in the
shabbiest of clothes, having alarming gaps in the legs
of his trousers, showing his bare leg at the knees, and
with large holes at his elbows. He came in on tiptoe
with his boots in his hand.

"Lor!" cried Froggy in great astonishment; "why,
its *Mac!*"

"Hold your tongue!" whispered Mac, putting his
finger to his lips as a sign to them to be quiet, and
jerking his thumb over his shoulder to indicate downstairs. "If the old mother catches me, there'll be no
end of a row. I've just stole up without my boots to
see 'ow you two chaps is getting on this weather, and
to put you up to a wrinkle or two in case you're
a'most starved."

Froggy and Benny stared at him in great alarm,
for they knew what terrible risk they were running by
having Mac in their garret. They knew that if Mrs
Ragbon came up, and found him there, she would
not only turn Mac out "neck and crop," but she
would turn *them* out also.

"Don't come, Mac," pleaded Froggy imploringly;
"we'll all catch it if you do."

"I heard a door bang then," said Benny, clinging to Froggy in fear lest the landlady had already
started on her way upstairs.

"Now don't be afeared," said Mac, relapsing into
a broad grin. "I watched the old woman out in her
bonnet and shawl afore ever I come. She's gone
round to see a friend, same as she allays did Sun-

days. *I* knows her ways, bless you ! I came up dark
cos o' the other lodgers—they might tell on me if
they see'd me ; but I didn't run up against no one, so
we're 'all serène'!"

Froggy and Benny were by no means satisfied, but
they saw it was no good urging upon Mac to leave,
for he had evidently made up his mind to stay. He
put down his boots, thrust his hands into his pockets,
and seated himself with an independent bump close
to the grate, where there was still a slight blaze
visible, as if he had every right to be there, and
had not the slightest intention of leaving for the
present.

"Well, now," he began, "I come to see how you two
chaps is getting on. I've often thought on you this
cold weather—ain't it cold just?" he said shivering,—
"and wondered what you was doing all along o'
yourselves ; for Jack told me you was a shifting
now alone. How are you off for food and that of a
day ?"

"Oh, middling," said Froggy, not at all comfortable in his mind yet about Mac, and wondering how
it would be possible to hide him if Mrs Ragbon did
come up.

"We gets on very bad indeed," declared little
Benny earnestly, thinking Froggy had not been half
strong enough in saying they got on "middling."
"We gets emptier and emptier, and all our little
ribs is sticking out. I've got a mouse, Mac,—a dear
little bootiful thing, that I loves next to Froggy ;

and sometimes we can't gid him not a crumb, cos we've got nothink to make the crumbs with."

"What 'ave you got there ? " asked Mac, nodding at the tea-table.

" A nerring ! " said Benny.

" Have some, Mac, if you're hungry," said Froggy, generously preparing to share his portion with Mac.

" No, thank you," said Mac, looking rather disdain-fully at the frizzled up tail-end of the little fish. " I knows where I can get better tackle than that. Lor' bless you ! *I*'m never hungry like you chaps. I'm leading a reg'lar merry life, and gets as much beer and grub as ever I could if I was a royal dook. But *I* don't go crossing-sweeping, tho' I did try it first when I went on my own hook. I very soon left it off, and took to somethink more paying, and I'm getting on capital now."

"What do you do?" asked Froggy, looking earnestly at Mac, thinking perhaps *he* might be able to follow the same paying business, if he knew what it was.

Mac looked as if he were uncertain what to answer exactly, but said, after a moment's consideration, " Well, I lives on my wits."

" What is wits ? " asked Benny.

" Well, wits is wits," said Mac, unable to furnish a better explanation. " I goes about keeping my weather-h'eye open, and turns my hand to anythink that'll bring me in a penny, and never loses a chance. For hinstance," he said, " me and a chap went last Derby Day to h'Epsom, and made a capital day of

it. Him and me, we dressed oursels up in billycock
hats, put on large paper collars, blacked our faces,
and played the bones, and sang 'Slap bang 'ere we
are again!' It took capital. We chaffed the swells
and sang to the ladies—

> ' Some lady's lost her chi-non,
> All plaited and the pin on ! "

and did the cheeky wherever we had the chance.
We got no end of coppers from parties just to get rid
of us, and one gent as was having lunch on the top of
a coach, ee threw us a bit of a fowl, and another gent
gave us half a cake and some rich pie stuff—lor'! how
good that was!—and Chick and me, we got a drink o'
water, and did as well in the eating line as the Prince
o' Wales hisself!"

The idea of Mac going about in a stick-up paper
collar and a billycock hat, with a blackened face,
seemed much to entertain Froggy and Benny, and
they were all eagerness for Mac to tell them some
more of his doings.

"Tell us some more what you've done?" said Benny.

"Well," said Mac, "there was that grand to-do of
the Thanksgiving, when the Queen went to St Paul's
after the Prince was took so bad and got well. We
did a tidy business that day, though Chick got into
trouble with the p'leece, and was took to the lock-up."

"What did he do wrong?" asked Froggy.

"Oh, nothink at all," said Mac, evidently unwilling
to enter into the particulars of his companion's disgrace; "ee was let free the next day. We got enough

Thanksgiving Day to keep us in plenty the whole winter. . Now wouldn't you sooner come along with me, and do the same as me, than go standing at that crossing all day, taking nothink ? "

" Yes, Mac, if I'd get some money along with you," said poor, half-starved Froggy.

" Then come along then ! " exclaimed Mac encouragingly. " There'll be a fine chance for doing some business, Wednesday; and you shall come along with me that day, and we'll share everythink we gets ; only you must promise to do everythink I tells you, without asking no questions—do you hear ? "

"Yes, Mac," said Froggy. "I won't ask you nothink. But what's going to be done, Wednesday ? "

" Why, you knows Victoria Park, don't you ? " said Mac. " Well, the Queen is comin to the h'East End purpose to see it, and drive through it, along with one o' the Princesses, and there'll be no end of a crowd and fuss."

" And will Froggy have to wear a billycock and stick-ups and 'ave his face black ? " inquired little Benny hoping very much he should have the fun of seeing Froggy start out in this guise.

" No, nothink o' that," replied Mac. " P'r'aps he'll have to sell some cigar-lights, and be ready at this kind o' thing, cos it comes in useful sometimes ; " and as Mac spoke he got up from his sitting posture, and quick as lightning went across the garret throwing somersaults one after the other, as if he

had not an atom of bone in his body. He looked
like some curious species of firework, with his
yellow head and bare knees and elbows visible
at intervals in his quick evolutions about the
garret; and little Benny opened his large mouth,
and fairly shouted with laughter. And Froggy
laughed too, in a soberer fashion, more indeed out
of sympathy with Benny, than from any real mirth
he had in his heart. He was so glad to see Benny
laughing, for Benny had not laughed heartily like
this for a long time, and Froggy had been pondering very sorrowfully of late over the fact that
"Benny didn't seem as merry as he used, cos he
never laughed."

They had forgotten all about Mrs Ragbon, and
Mac was in the middle of a somersault, when suddenly a great noise and slamming of doors was
heard downstairs, and Mac paused to listen with
a leg in the air, just as he would be before turning
right over, and one hand on the ground. A deep
silence fell on the whole party, for the landlady's
voice was heard scolding loudly below, and in
another minute her heavy footstep was heard un-
mistakably creaking upstairs. She was calling
out in a tone of hottest anger, as step by step she
ascended, "I'll catch you, you young rascal you!
I knows where you are—don't you think I don't
know where you are now!" and it was evident
she carried a stick with her, for she was sounding
it against the stairs, in order, no doubt, to strike

E

terror into the heart of the "young rascal" whom
she was promising to catch, and who, of course,
was Mac.

Froggy and Benny became white with terror,
absolutely at a loss to imagine the dreadful scene
that would occur between the wrathful mother
and her son; but Mac was as cool as possible.
He gazed at the door fixedly for one moment, to
make sure she was coming, in an attitude of defiant
impudence, with his thumb to his nose, and his
tongue out; then, with the quickness of his class,
so accustomed to outwitting the police and dodging
the School Board officers, he jumped on· to the mattress whereon Froggy and Benny slept, pulled the
clothes over him, and lay so still and flat that no
one entering could possibly have imagined there
could be a human being lying underneath. In
another second the door flew open, and in burst
Mrs Ragbon. Glancing rapidly round the garret,
and seeing no Mac, she became furious.

"The young rascal!" she exclaimed; "if he
hasn't give me the slip after all. He's in the house,
I know he is! Thompson said he saw him come
in not ten minutes ago, and if he's up the chimney,
I'll fetch him down, as sure as my name's Sal
Ragbon!" She delivered herself of this speech
apparently unmindful of the two poor little boys
cowering close together over the fire, upon whose
privacy she had thus abruptly intruded.

The garret was so bare of furniture and hiding-places of any kind, that Mrs Ragbon, after taking the first searching look around, became satisfied that she was on the wrong scent, and that Mac could not be there, but must be down in one of the other rooms. The mattress was spread close to the floor, so that there was no bed to look *under*, and *in* it, fortunately, it never occurred to her to look, though Froggy and Benny were literally trembling with fear lest she should suddenly take it into her head to stalk forward and give the mattress a sounding rap with her stick, which would have roused Mac with a start and a scream, and then what a scene there would have been! How Mac would have fought! and how Mrs Ragbon would have fought! and who can tell what might have happened?

Such a scene would indeed have been painful and dreadful to witness between mother and son, between whom Christ Himself has taught us, both by precept and example, that there should ever be the deepest reverence and the holiest love. Christ never preached what He did not practise; and mark, little children, how kind He always was to His mother; how, when He hung bleeding on the cross for our sins, almost His last thought was for her, when He said to that disciple whom He loved, "Behold thy mother!" thus providing an earthly home for her after He was gone. There is no sin more grievous in Christ's eyes than that of rebelliousness towards parents. Whatever may be

our parents' failings and shortcomings, we are bound
to love, honour, and succour them.

Mrs Ragbon was not a good mother; her passion
for drink, and her constant indulgence of it, had
drowned all her better feelings, her love for her
husband, and the duty she owed to her children;
but then Mac should not have been rude and dis-
obedient to her. That was not being a good son.
He should have worked hard, and tried to win his
mother back again by leading a good life himself,
and being kind; and who can tell that, with God's
blessing, he might not have succeeded?

Having satisfied herself that Mac was not in the
garret, the landlady, anxious not to lose time, turned
on her heel directly, and went scolding down to the
lower regions in search of him. The moment the
door closed, down went the clothes, and up jumped
Mac.

"Slap bang 'ere we are again!" he said, springing
to his feet, and laughing as if he thought it a capital
joke.

"O Mac! however will you get out?" exclaimed
Froggy, not laughing at all, but very grave and
frightened.

"Well, I must watch my chance, same as I've
often done before," replied Mac, moving towards the
door and cautiously opening it. "Listen!" he said,
with his finger up, and peeping down the dark stairs,
"she's gone into mother Blunt's now, and lor'! what
a row she's making! She wants to look in the

saucepan for me, and they won't let her, and there!
she's just given one of the brats *such* a knock, don't
you hear him squealing? I must make a dash in a
minute. 'Ere, Benny, give me my boots."

Benny handed them to him tremblingly, with his
poor little white face looking quite scared at the
danger Mac was in.

"O Mac! do take care!" entreated Froggy. "If
she finds out you've bin here, she'll come up and
beat Benny and me—I knows she will, Mac!"

"Don't be afraid. *I* won't get you into any
hobble, not me!" returned Mac assuringly. "Now
don't forget Wednesday. Be up early, and meet
me at the top of the street, mind."

With these words, he rubbed his hands as if
bracing himself up for action, and then suddenly
dashing forward, took a flying leap downstairs, past
Mrs Blunt's door, down some more stairs, along the
passage, and out at the street-door, before Mrs
Ragbon could possibly catch him, though she was
just in time to see his yellow head disappearing
from her premises. She ran out into the street
calling out loudly "Police! police!" but Froggy
and Benny, watching from their garret window, saw
Master Mac turn the corner, and they knew then
that he had made good his escape, and that neither
Mrs Ragbon nor the police would be able to catch
him.

CHAPTER VI.

FROGGY GOES OUT WITH MAC.

 N the morning of the day on which our gracious Queen did an act of kindness which sent happiness and sunshine into the hearts and homes of thousands of her poor subjects in the toiling East End, by coming amongst them, and driving through their Park, there was a great stir going on in the garrets and kitchens and first-floor backs and fronts in Shoreditch. The inhabitants of this neighbourhood are habitually early risers, but they were earlier than ever this morning, and seemed to be unanimous in their desire to get some extra time before the work-a-day world usually awoke, so that they might be free later. They all felt that this was to be no ordinary day. There was a wide-spread and a very happy feeling abroad that the Queen was coming to see them each personally, and therefore it behoved them, as affectionate and loyal subjects, to go forth into the streets and greet her, as many as could. For this reason, fathers were content to make shift at their breakfasts, and to help in a great many little household matters which they generally left to their wives to do, because they knew that Mary Anne or Betsy Jane was busy tidying up the children, and giving them an extra wash under the pump in preparation for the holiday. And oh ! how happy the children were because mother was going to take them to see the Queen ! They were to be lifted out of the gutter for one short day, and taken out into the open streets, away from the wretched alleys and close courts and passages, into lighter and purer air ; and oh ! delight of delights !—mother had told them that when the Queen went by, they might "Hip-hip hooray !" as loud as ever they liked, and make as much noise as they could !

The cold grey light of the dawn was just stealing in at the garret window when Benny, rubbing his eyes with his small fists, woke up, and was surprised to find no Froggy lying by his side. Rising up on his elbow, he looked out upon the garret, and then discovered Froggy in one corner, standing over a tub washing himself, with his little thin spider-like body shivering with cold, and his head looking like the top of a mop, as he kept plunging it in the water, and then bringing it out again with a jerk.

"Froggy, 'ow quick you is up !" exclaimed Benny.

"Yes, cos I've got to meet Mac, don't you know ? " said Froggy, burying his wet face as he spoke in a tattered thing he called a towel. "This is Wednesday morning. I'm glad you've woke, cos I want to practise my tumbling;" and forthwith he began throwing somersaults as fast as he could about the garret, and making Benny laugh and rub his hands with delight.

"You do it cap'ly," said he when Froggy had done, and stood panting with the exertion, "as well as Mac did. I wish, Froggy, *I* was going to see the Queen too."

"Do you?" said Froggy. "Well, go along with Jack—ee's sure to be going."

"I'll try," said Benny in a tone that showed he was a little doubtful of Jack's taking him. "I *would* like to see her, and the soldiers, and hear the music and everythink, that I would! Do you think, Froggy, she'll be in a gold carriage, and wear a crown, and look like the queen on the pennies—do you, Froggy?"

"I think she'll wear a bonnet, same as the grand ladies does in the parks," replied Froggy, "but I'm not quite sure o' that. You must take care you isn't run over in the crowd. We've got nothink of a breakfast to call a breakfast," said he, regarding the few dry crusts which represented the larder; "but you know what Mac said; we was sure to get on to-day, and he'd share everythink with me. So we shall 'ave a good supper to-night, Benny, and p'r'aps be able to 'ave a fire and get warm."

After this the two boys ate their crusts, and Benny having dressed, threw himself on the ground, and coaxed the mouse out of his hole to eat the crumbs he had taken care to leave. Froggy gave his little

brother a kiss, and told him to be a good boy if he
went out with Jack, and then sallied forth into the
streets to meet his companions for the day. Froggy
wandered up and down for a long time before Mac
appeared. When at last he did appear, he was not
alone, but was accompanied by two boys, whom
Froggy scrutinised with great interest. They were
curious-looking individuals, possibly of thirteen or
fourteen, with apparently boy's bodies and men's
heads. They wore their hair closely shaven, and
they had shrewd restless little eyes, that seemed
capable of taking in a thousand things at once.
Froggy thought at one minute they *must* be old men,
grown down from age; then again that they must
be boys after all, because of their small hands and
feet, and their little chests and backs. Mac called
one Chickabiddy and the other Dandy. They eyed
Froggy sharply when they met, as if they would like
to get inside of him if they could, to see what he was
made of.

"Is he pretty quick?" asked Dandy of Mac,
regarding Froggy as if he were some new little
animal brought into market to be discussed.

"Yes, middling," said Mac. "He'll do for what
we wants."

"He's quite fresh, ain't he?" said Chickabiddy in
an undertone.

"Yes, *very*," replied Mac with emphasis; and then
the three turned abruptly with one accord, and
walked together straight ahead, because Chickabiddy

intimated the approach of a policeman, and they all seemed anxious to get out of his way.

Froggy followed them silently down a great many streets and through crowded courts and alleys, and many queer places where he had never been before, wondering to himself a good deal the while where Chickabiddy and Dandy came from—how old they really were—whether they were brothers, or only "mates"—how Mac had come to know them—what they did to earn their bread—and a thousand other things. He heard them talking together as they went along in rather mysterious language at times, using expressions he did not understand, and which evidently had reference to the day's proceedings. They seemed to be marking out a plan of action for themselves, in which Froggy soon saw he was intended to play a part; for Dandy kept alluding to "that there!" and Chickabiddy to the "colt!" with various signs and nods, which left no doubt in Froggy's mind that he was the "that there" and "the colt" indicated. Whenever a policeman came in sight, Froggy noticed they avoided meeting him if possible—sometimes by crossing to the other side, or slipping down a side street. Now and then they parted company, and each went different ways, as if they did not desire to be seen together, but always meeting again shortly afterwards, and continuing their conversation.

By and by they got into the line of streets through which the Queen was going to pass on her way to

Victoria Park. Everywhere along the royal route there was a tremendous crowd assembling, though it was yet early in the day. Men, women, and children lined the kerbstones, jostling one another for a front place, determined to stand there till they dropped rather than not get a sight of their Queen. There were policemen keeping order amongst the crowd, and directing the traffic—now battling with a refractory costermonger who wanted to go his own way, now helping a heavily-burdened mother with a perambulator across the road—now collaring a pick-pocket—now telling a suspicious character to "move on," &c., &c. There were ragged men with greasy hats and shoeless feet pattering up and down the muddy road in and out of the crowd, calling out in sharp, metallic voices, "Only *one* ape'ny! portrait of 'er Majesty Queen Victoria in her crownation robes! *honly* one ape'ny!" and there were others of the same unwholesome fraternity selling rattles and whistles, and cardboard carriages, and "Jump Jim Crows" dangling at the end of elastic, and hosts of other wares, all at the same tempting price of " *h'only* one ape'ny!" There were the provision sellers too—men with trays full of brandy-balls and penny packets of ginger-nuts, speckled profusely with almond; and at the corners of the streets, wher-ever the police permitted them to be, there were Punch and Judy shows, and "happy families," and acrobats in velvet dresses and spangles, and many other performances, which seldom exhibited in these parts except on such a rare occasion as this, when the Queen was coming, and there was a large crowd to amuse.

The poor East End seemed to be quite agog with excitement, and every moment the crowd became greater.

About an hour before the Queen was expected, Chickabiddy, Dandy, and Mac pulled up at a point where the crowd was densest, and Froggy heard Dandy say approvingly, "Yes, I thinks this'll do as well as any!" There was evidently the fullest understanding between these three, and though Chickabiddy and Dandy now nodded to Mac, and went off in different directions amongst the crowd, Froggy felt their partnership was by no means dissolved.

"Now, Frog, lookee here," said Mac; "don't you take no notice of me, but do just as I tell you. Do you see that old party with blue spectacles and a big chain opposite?'

"Yes," said Froggy.

"Well, now," said Mac, "you go across and begin tumbling in front of him. Keep turning head-over-heels until I tell you to stop. Mind you 'tract his attention, and after a bit, ask him to shy you a copper. Don't take 'No' for a hanser, but go on till he turns reg'lar crusty, or I beckons to you to leave off."

Froggy, who had promised on Sunday, you know, to obey Mac without asking questions, went across

"Well, now," said Mac, "you go across and begin tumbling in front of him, keep turning head-over-heels until I tell you to stop."

and did exactly what Mac had told him. He began turning somersaults in the muddy road right in front of the old gentleman Mac had pointed out. He was a very kind, benevolent-looking old gentleman, taking care of several children, who, when Froggy commenced his performances, called out gleefully—

"Look, grandpa, dear! look at that funny little boy. Won't he get splashed in the mud, and won't he get giddy turning over like that?"

"I should think his mother will give him a thrashing when he gets home," said the grandpapa, "for getting his clothes so dirty."

"Please, grandpa, dear! throw him a penny," said one of the little children, "because I think he's doing it for us."

The grandpapa began fumbling at once, first in one pocket and then in another, for some halfpence he knew he had, and at last flung a penny into the road to Froggy. Froggy was just in the act of picking it up, when he was surprised by feeling a very heavy hand laid on his shoulder, and looking up, he saw a tall policeman regarding him sternly over his stiff collar.

"What is it, sir, please?" asked Froggy, very much frightened, for he had never been taken hold of by a policeman in this way before.

"I can't allow you to be doing this here," said the policeman; "you must move on. You are out along with some others, aren't you?"

"Yes, sir," answered Froggy truthfully at once.

" I'm out along with that chap there !" pointing to
Mac, who a minute before had been dodging mysteriously behind the old gentleman, but who was
now standing at a short distance from him, looking
moodily out to the left, as if he were out on no particular business whatever.

"Ah! I thought so!" said the policeman. "*I'll* keep
my eye on you, you young rascals you!" and giving
Froggy an admonishing shake and a push forward, he
released him, and went across the road to assist at a
cab accident which had just occurred.

Then Froggy saw Mac beckon to him, and immediately after Chickabiddy and Dandy, whom Froggy
had not seen for some time, came up and joined Mac,
and together with him began interrogating Froggy
strictly as to what the policeman had said to him.

" He asked me if I was out along with other chaps,"
said Froggy.

" And what did you say ? " asked Dandy quickly.

"Yes, I said I was with him," replied Froggy,
pointing to Mac.

" You *was* a flat ! " said Chickabiddy, with his old
man's face looking wrathfully contemptuous.

"Yes, that you was!" said Mac. "Now, just recollect this : if a policeman asks you again, you are to
say, 'No, you're not out with nobody;' do you hear ? "

" Yes," said Froggy; but the moment he had said
" Yes," he was very sorry, for it was consenting to an
untruth ; and Froggy was, of all things, a truthful
boy. Before he had time to recall it, Dandy said—

"Well, let's come on now as we're spotted. We'd better go to old Solomon's, and have somethink to drink."

Chickabiddy and Mac seemed quite to agree, and without more talking they all walked briskly off, and went down a side street, which led to a dingy quarter, where there were old tumbledown shops, and not many people about. When they were well out of the crowd, Froggy saw Chickabiddy sidle close up to Mac, and open his hand just wide enough to let him see that in the palm lay a large silver watch.

"What a lovely!" exclaimed Mac.

"Solomon 'll give you a lot for that," said Dandy. "Now, Mac, what 'ave you got?"

"I'm down in my luck to-day," said Mac; "I've only got two o' these," showing the corner of a very voluminous white pocket-handkerchief.

Froggy wondered to himself very much how they had got these things, and was just on the point of asking, when they stopped at the door of a dingy little shop, over which hung three golden balls, which Froggy knew to be the pawnbroker's sign. And into this shop they all went one after another, telling Froggy he was to remain outside. Froggy could see through the open door that the shop was full of old clothes, and that there was a very old man, with a hooked nose and a hump on his back, sitting behind the counter, who was evidently that "old Solomon" whom Dandy had spoken about, for he heard Chickabiddy say as he entered, "How do do, old Sol?"

There appeared to be a great talking and bargaining for a few minutes, then they issued forth again into the street in very high spirits.

"Sol's behaved like a reg'lar trump this time," remarked Dandy to his friends, chinking some money in his right hand.

"Now for something to drink!" said Chickabiddy gaily.

"Here, Frog!" said Mac, handing him two shillings, "'ere's a couple o' bob for you! What do you say to that, young 'un? ain't that rather better than sweeping a crossin, eh?"

"I dunno," said Froggy rather bluntly; then, looking straight up into Mac's face, he asked, "Where did you and your mates get them things from, Mac?"

"Didn't I tell you you was to ask no questions?" returned Mac severely. "Take your couple o' bob and be thankful!"

"We picks 'em up as we goes along," said Chickabiddy with a chuckle; and then they crossed the road, and went into a public-house, where they refreshed themselves with great tankards of beer and sausage rolls. They all drank and ate, except Froggy, who said he didn't want any—he'd rather keep his money.

"Oh, I knows why that is," said Mac. "You're thinking of the little chap at home, and buyin' coals and food, and that like. But you shall 'ave another two bob before the day is over, bless you! Come, have some beer!"

"No, I don't wants it," said Froggy resolutely, and he kept true to his resolution.

Froggy was very hungry and very thirsty, and the sight of the beer and refreshment was very tempting to him, but there was an extremely uneasy feeling in Froggy's mind that his companions had not come by their gains lawfully, and that he ought not to keep the money Mac had given him. At any rate, he made up his mind not to spend any of it at present. He would keep his eyes open very sharply for the rest of the day, and try to discover, if he could, how Mac really did become possessed of such very large white silk pocket-handkerchiefs; for he was not quite so simple as to believe entirely Chickabiddy's statement, "that they picked them up as they went along." Putting two and two together, he became more than ever convinced that his suspicions were correct, for if Mac and the others had been honest, why should the policeman have said, "Ah! he'd keep his eye on them all!" and why should Mac have objected to his telling the policeman the truth?

After their refreshment, the boys walked much farther afield, and did not stop again till they got into the crowd waiting about the entrance of Victoria Park. Then they pulled up, and dispersed as they had done before, and Mac told Froggy to begin tumbling in the mud, and asking certain people whom he pointed out to Froggy "to shy him coppers!"

Froggy had scarcely begun, when there was a great

F

flutter and movement in the crowd, everybody
pressing closer to the kerb, and showing great
excitement, for in the distance they could hear the
people cheering, and it was evident now that the
Queen was approaching! The police woke to greater
activity, hustling every kind of obstruction out of the
roadway, and making short work of anybody or anything which showed signs of resistance. One policeman collared Froggy, and sent him reeling on to the
pavement, and it was some minutes before he regained his breath, and recovered the shaking. When
he looked up rather disturbed and red in the face, he
saw Mac not far off, and Mac was looking at him and
laughing as much as to say, "Didn't you get a
shaking that time, old fellow?"

A few minutes passed, and then the moment of
excitement arrived. The sun shone out, some outriders in scarlet appeared, and then came the royal
carriage, containing the Queen and the Princess
Beatrice, who were smiling graciously, and bowing
right and left to the crowd, in acknowledgment of the
hearty salutations which greeted them. The women
waved their hands, the men cheered lustily, and the
children roared "Hip, hip, hooray!" till they were
hoarse. Froggy had a capital view, and hoorayed at
the top of his voice with the rest. He wondered
where Benny was, and hoped he was seeing well too!

As soon as the Queen had passed, there was great
confusion in the crowd; some people rushing to keep
up with the royal carriage, others rushing off home-

wards now the sight was over in a contrary direction,
and there were a great many old people turning
about with a dazed look, as if the noise and rush had
bewildered them, and they did not know exactly
where they were going, or what was the next thing to
be done. These of course got into the way of everybody, who had any fixed plans of action, and so
everybody seemed to think it fair to give them a
push, and send them on a few steps, whether they
liked it or not.

Froggy especially noticed one old gentleman, who
was moving about in this undecided sort of way, and
who was getting a good deal hustled by his more
strong-minded neighbours. Watching him, Froggy
became aware that Mac was watching the old
gentleman too. Mac seemed to be hovering at the
back of him, and so were Chickabiddy and Dandy in
front. Why were they all looking so keen and
mysterious? What were they after? thought Froggy.
He determined now to keep his eye on them and find
out. Presently Froggy saw Chickabiddy go up and
ask the old gentleman the time, which seemed to
startle the old gentleman, and flurry him very much.
While he was fumbling and diving for his watch,
which lived deep down in a waistcoat pocket, Froggy
observed Mac steal quietly up at the back, and
sheltered by Dandy on one side, deliberately put
his hand in the old gentleman's pocket, and
draw out his yellow silk handkerchief! There!
Froggy saw it all now—he saw what Chickabiddy and

Dandy and Mac were; they were *thieves!* He had
suspected it, and now he knew it. Oh, how hot and
ashamed and degraded poor Froggy felt! he wished
a thousand times he had never come out with Mac;
he wished he had stayed at his crossing or stayed in
the garret with Benny; anything would have been
better than this! What would the gentleman think
who had taught him at the night-school if he could
know he had been the companions of thieves and
pickpockets all day! and oh! what would father and
mother think if they were looking down at him from
their home in heaven! This thought filled Froggy's
eyes with tears, and a great sorrow came into his
heart; a longing to be dead, and to be with them,
out of the sin and misery and temptation of this
world, in that other one, where there is no struggling
for daily bread, and where nobody has to pay for
their lodging!

Froggy was feeling something of that craving
for deep rest, which is natural for old men and
old women to feel after they have been tossing
on the waves of this troublesome world for a lifetime, but which is very sad to see in a child. Froggy
was but eleven, and he should not have been feeling
like an old tired man; at this rate, what would his
heart be like at forty? London has nothing more
sorrowful to show us, I think, amongst all its sorrowful sights, than its old children, with their
shrewd, anxious faces, and knitted brows, on which
hard Care is stamped, instead of the glad expec-

tancy and joyous carelessness which we generally associate with childhood.

Immediately after securing the old gentleman's pocket-handkerchief, Mac and his companions walked off, and for a moment or two Froggy lost sight of them in the crowd. He had the two shillings still in his pocket, which Mac had given him after their visit to the pawnbroker's, and now he knew he ought to go to Mac, and give them back to him. They were *stolen* shillings, and knowing them to be stolen, would he not be quite as guilty of theft as Mac if he kept them? Froggy knew, of course, that he would be, and though the temptation was strong to keep them, *very* strong when he thought of Benny's white face and the empty garret at home, he resisted it, and determined to follow Mac, and return them to him at once.

He soon caught sight of Mac's yellow head bobbing in and out amongst the people a little distance in front of him, and he could see that Chickabiddy and Dandy were with him too. Froggy began to run, and got up with them just in time to see them all tumble into a public-house together, at the corner of the street. As the great door swung to in his face, poor Froggy, with a very heavy heart, took up his position outside to wait for them till they came out. Presently Dandy appeared looking rather weak about the knees, and extremely vacant, then Chickabiddy and Mac, looking quite as weak, but more cheerful.

" Lawksh ! " cried Chickabiddy, when he saw
Froggy. "'Ere's the frog run up ! "

" Mac," said Froggy going up to him, " here's
your two bob back again—I don't wants 'em."

Mac gazed at him with a stupid grin, and seemed
not to understand what he said.

" Mac," repeated Froggy louder, thrusting the
money into his hand, " take your two bob back
again, I say. I'd rather starve than steal, and I
know you've stole 'em ! You're all of you *thiefs*,
and I don't wants to speak to you again ! "

Their understandings were all more or less clouded
by drink, but they understood Froggy's words pretty
well, and saw by his manner, and the set of his little
shoulders, that he was saying things the reverse of
complimentary to them.

They were just in the condition to enjoy a scrim-
mage of any kind, and so they closed round Froggy,
and began knocking him about as hard as they
could, waxing warmer as their blows became harder.
Froggy was a plucky little fellow, and struck out
gallantly with arms and legs, back and front and
to the sides of him (for he was attacked by his
cowardly assailants at all points), and at last succeeded in giving Dandy a tremendous black eye,
and to the other two such kicks and blows, as to
disable them for a moment, and then Froggy
thought he would make his escape before they
could renew their attack. He could not afford
to fight longer, because his jacket was getting

torn to pieces, being ragged already, and then he had not the strength for it either, for he had had no beer and sausage-rolls to sustain him as his antagonists had had, and he was feeling faint for want of food. So, having shaken himself free, he marched on down the street, taking very long, independent strides, and not once looking back, though he knew Mac and the others were trying to follow him. But they were all too hopelessly the worse for drinking to make much way, and in a few minutes Froggy had left them far behind, reeling and staggering amongst the crowd.

Froggy never forgot his little brother by any chance, and he began to think what he should take home to Benny for his supper. He had, alas! only one penny to spend, but that would buy something. After much consideration he decided upon buying two meat-pies which he saw in a cook-shop, marked a halfpenny each, because they were stale. Benny would not mind their being stale, and the two would make him quite a sumptuous meal; and Froggy thought perhaps he himself might take just a quarter of one, as he was so hungry! But he wouldn't take more—of that he was determined. It was quite a "catch," in Froggy's opinion, to have got these pies,. and he pursued his way homewards for some time after, with a much lighter heart.

By and by a strange sensation crept over Froggy —an overpowering feeling of faintness, and the cabs and omnibuses in the road, and the people all about

him, seemed to him to be whirling round and round.
He made his way to a doorstep, where he sat down
to recover himself, and there, poor little weary fellow !
he fell fast asleep, and dreamed that he was a little
boy again (for he thought he was an old man now)
taken caré of by his mother and father, as he used
to be when they had the Punch and Judy show,
and Benny was a baby. He dreamed he was in
his little night-shirt sitting on his mother's knee,
and she was rocking him to sleep with her arms
round him, and singing to him a soft lullaby, as
she used often to do, after they had had a long
day out at the West End, and Froggy had been
a good boy, and "walked out brave!" Oh! for
those blessed, happy days, when mother used to
sing to him lullabies !—Froggy woke up with a
little sob, because he knew it was all a dream,
and, opening his eyes wide, he saw the streets
were now dark. The lamps were all lit, and the
gas was flaring in the butchers' and green-grocers'
shops. "It must be evening, and Benny must
have gone home some time!" he thought. Jumping up from the doorstep with an overtaken look,
he made his way hurriedly through the busy streets,
never once stopping till he reached the blackened
house in Shoreditch, which was his home.

" He dreamed he was in his little night-shirt sitting on his mother's knee."

CHAPTER VII.

FROGGY WRITES TO THE QUEEN.

WHILE Froggy was on the doorstep, Benny was at home, seated on the topmost step of the stairs just outside the garret, waiting for Froggy. His little heart was full of eager expectation at his coming, because he imagined such great things would result from this long day out with Mac. He was depending upon a fire for one thing to warm his poor little body by, and perhaps something hot for supper as soon as Froggy came home, and perhaps Froggy might bring money in his pocket as well to pay for some candles, and some wood, and some oatmeal, and all the other things they were so much in need of. While he was sitting there alone in the dark, the woman who lodged below came out on to the landing to fetch some wood in, and turning her head upwards, perceived by the light of her candle, that there was something seated at the top of the stairs. She paused for a moment and then called out—

"Is that you, Benny, up there, or the cat?"

Benny thought he would pretend to be the cat, so he answered demurely—

" Me-yow ! me-yow ! "

" Oh, you little rascal you ! " called back the downstairs lodger good-temperedly. " You can't do me like that—I know its *Benny !*—Why, isn't your brother come back yet, Benny ? "

" No," said Benny, patiently. " But I'm sure he won't be long now. I specs to hear 'im open the door every minute."

" Haven't you got a bit o' candle to light up with ? " said the woman.

" No—we's quite out o' lights," answered the little voice from the darkness, then hopefully, "but Froggy'll bring some when he comes."

Mrs Blunt, for that was the lodger's name, disappeared into her room for a minute, and then came out again with half a rushlight, and a match in her hand, which she held out to Benny.

" There ! that'll last till you go to bed," she said.

" Thank you, mum," said little Benny, sliding cautiously down the steep steps to take the gift, and then quickly mounting again to resume his seat on the top of the stairs. He was very much surprised, and very pleased, for Mrs Blunt was not in the habit of giving them things. She had a hard struggle to get on herself, with half-a-dozen children about her, and a drunken husband to boot. She went out as charwoman during the day, and took in washing as well when she could get it; yet with all her exertions, she could barely pay her rent. She was always behindhand with it, and was being constantly threatened with a visit from the brokers, by the unmerciful landlady, Mrs Ragbon. So she had it not in her power to be very generous to the two little boys above her, though she felt very kindly towards them. She knew they suffered bitterly, like all the rest of that unhappy household, and they had no mother to teach them what was right, and what was wrong, and yet they were so honest! She had never missed a bundle of wood during the whole winter, though the temptation to steal a few sticks must have been often great, for the poor charwoman kept her little store just outside the door in a small heap, in full view of their eyes, whenever they passed up or down.

Benny thought he wouldn't light up till Froggy came, "cos maybe the light mayn't last us till we gets to bed," said he to his prudent little self, as he sat there all in the dark again after Mrs Blunt had gone into her room, and shut the door.

"I wish we was like the cats, I does, cos they sees in the dark, and they don't want no candles, nor clothes neither, cos they're born with nice little fur trousers on their legs, and warm little coats on their backs, what never gets torn, and they don't 'ave to pay no rent like Froggy and me does. I wish I was a cat! I wonder if Froggy 'ud like to be a cat too. I think I'd have my tail cut off, then nobody could pull it, I'd never go after the mouses, and I'd never,

oh I'd never if I was a cat, go into anybody's room,
and take the meat, like Mr Tom did to we, when
Froggy and me was savin' a nice little bit for supper.
That was so mean of Tom, so sly! I haven't give
him a beating for it, cos Froggy said I wasn't, but I
sure he specs one."

Benny left off thinking about cats now, for he
heard the street door go, and he made up his mind it
was Froggy come at last! He jumped up from his
perch at once, and ran into the damp dark garret,
where he struck the match, and set it to the rushlight, which cast a feeble gleam down the ricketty
stairs, up which Froggy was slowly labouring.

"He's comin' very slow!" thought Benny, with his
little heart quite beating with happy excitement;
"but maybe he's weighed down wid all the coals and
meat and things, and can't get up quick!"

Another moment, and Froggy appeared. At the
very first sight of him all the joy fled out of Benny's
heart! What was the meaning of his torn jacket,
and his pale dejected face, which looked like that of
a suffering old man when the yellow gleam of the
rushlight fell upon it! Benny eyed him gravely for
one moment, and then said anxiously—

"Froggy, darlin', you've not never bin fightin', has
you?"

"Yes, I has," said Froggy mournfully. "I've had a
reg'lar big fight with Mac, and two other chaps;" and
then he sat down on the mattress, and Benny could
see that large tears were trickling down his cheeks,

which greatly distressed Benny, because Froggy so
seldom cried, and he knew he must be very unhappy
to do so.

"Don't cry, Froggy," said little Benny comfortingly,
making a very funny face as he spoke, with his nose
and eyes and mouth all working at different angles
in the effort to keep back his own tears, which were
rising in sympathy with Froggy's; "I's *so* sorry!
Hasn't the day bin good, Froggy? didn't you tumble
to please Mac? what made 'im fight you, and them
others—eh, Froggy?"

"Cos I wouldn't *thieve* like they!" answered Froggy
scornfully. "Mac and his mates they're pickpockets.
I found that out, and cos I wouldn't touch none o'
their money, they began cuffin me about, and then
my monkey got up, and we fought, and they've tore
my jacket between 'em!" looking ruefully over his
shoulder, where his little. shirt was bulging from a
great rent in his jacket.

"Poor Froggy!" said Benny in profound pity;
"you shall have *my* coat, Froggy—the coat what's in
the box. It's too long and too big for me, ain't it?
Don't you know you always says I looks like a little
old man Punch in it?" and he laughed out, in the
hope of cheering Froggy into a laugh too; but Froggy
was far too sad to laugh even a little to-night.

"I'm not cast down cos o' my jacket," he said,
looking out into the dreary garret with wide-opened
anxious eyes. "I'm thinkin as how I can't get food for
you, Benny, and we shall have to go into the House."

He covered his face with his hands, and Benny knew he was shedding bitter tears. Benny gulped down a sob himself at the thought of going to that terrible place, the workhouse, of which he had always heard the neighbours speak with such horror and dread, as if being driven to "the House" would be the very last sorrow and degradation they could know in their poor lives.

"There's nobody what'll help us—we've got no friends," said Froggy. "We may starve up here, and nobody'll care!"

"Oh yes, Froggy, darlin'—Gentle Jesus will care," said Benny. "I know He will, and He'll never let us starve if we ask Him. Don't you 'member, Froggy, about the little sparrows in the Bible? how God takes care of 'em, cos they can't take care o' themselves, and maybe He'll take care o' we!"

"Yes," said Froggy, beginning to dry up his tears at the thought of that Father in heaven, who clothes the lilies of the field, and who will not let even a little sparrow fall to the ground without Him. "Mother used to say that to father often when times was bad, and he talked o' 'the House,' and they was never driv to go there after all, never! God always took care of 'em."

Froggy was evidently comforted, and gaining heart again.

"I got you two pies," said Froggy, bringing them forth, and giving them to his little brother.

"I couldn't eat *both*," said Benny, nodding his head;

"deed I couldn't;" and he was so determined upon taking only one, that Froggy was forced to take the other.

Benny sat himself down on the floor close to Froggy, and for a few minutes they were silently engaged over their pies, as if satisfying such hunger as theirs was a very serious matter indeed.

"Did you see the Queen?" asked Benny when he had finished his pie and fed his mouse.

"Oh yes," said Froggy, "and the Princess, and the h'outriders in red, and everythink. Did you get a good sight out along with Jack?"

"I didn't go," said Benny, "Jack wouldn't take me; he said I must be like the little pig what didn't go to market, but stayed at home, and cried out wee! wee! wee! What is the Queen like, Froggy?"

"Oh such a kind-looking lady," said Froggy, "not a bit grand like, nor stuck up, but quite smiling and haffable, as if she war quite pleased to come, and 'ave a look at us. Oh my! how the people did ip! ip! ooray her!"

"Did she wear a crown on her head?" asked Benny.

"No—she wore a black bonnet, something like the ladies wears in church Sundays," said Froggy. "And, lor', she did look kind in it! A sort of a lady that with all the hearls, and lords, and dooks about 'er, wouldn't be too mighty to think of little chaps like we, if she knowed we was hungry and put to it!"

"O Froggy!" cried Benny, his face lighting up with a sudden inspiration. "Can't we write to the Queen, and tell 'er all about it?"

He waited breathless for one moment to see what Froggy would say.

"I wonder if the postman ud take it," said Froggy, ponderingly, and colouring up a little at the audacity of the plan.

"Oh yes, if we was to wrap it up neat, and put Bucknam Palace on the outside, and wrote it was for the Queen, and slipped it in the box, it ud sure to go," said Benny, as if there couldn't be a doubt about it.

"Then we'll write afore ever we goes to bed," said Froggy. "It's a good job I went to night-school and learnt how to write, ain't it?"

Benny's face clouded over for a moment, as if he had thought of some great obstacle.

"But, Froggy," he said, "whatever are we to do for paper and the hink?"

"Oh, I knows," said Froggy; and he crossed the garret to a dark corner, where there was a small square box standing, which had belonged to Froggy's father and mother. He untied the string which fastened it, and opening the lid, told Benny to bring the light, because he was going to hunt for something. He dived right to the bottom, and brought up a little blue bottle, in which there was some dried ink, then he found an old steel pen, and lastly between the leaves of his mother's Bible (which he used to read to Benny on Sundays) a sheet of white paper and an envelope which had grown yellow from long keeping.

"There! we've got everythink," said Froggy, shutting down the box, and making it fast again. " A drop of water to the ink is all we wants now." .

The drop of water was soon got, and in a few minutes the little brothers were seated over the rush-light in the middle of the garret, with their heads close together, and their minds wholly engrossed, writing their letter to the Queen.

There were many difficulties at starting; first to know how it would be proper to address her Majesty, Froggy being dreadfully afraid of being "too familiar." Then there were words to spell, which puzzled Froggy greatly, his learning having become a little rusty, since he no longer went to the night-school, and he had great trouble in forming some of the letters. But each difficulty was overcome in its turn, and at last, after much toil and perseverance, the following letter was written. It began—

LADY QUEEN,—We are two little brothers what lives in Shoreditch. We've got no money, and no friends. We lives in a garret. Mothers dead, and fathers dead, and Froggy, thats me, doesn't know how to get food for Benny, whos a littler chap, and my brother. Unless it was in the Bible about the little sparrows, we should amost think God was agoin to let us starve. They say you are a kind lady, and you looks kind, cos I seen you in your

G

potograts in the shop-winders, and I sees you to-day
agoin to the Park, along with the Princess, a-smilin
quite as if you knowed us all, and was a-askin us
how we did about coals and vittals and things, now that
them things is so dear. Benny and mes quite out of
em, and we've got no breakfast to-morrow, nor no
money neither, and we're afraid as how we shall have
to go into the House, which some folks says is worse
than prisons. If you ask Mrs Blunt, she'll tell you
it's all true—she's the lodger what lives underneath."

Here the letter ended, because the rushlight began
to sputter and to shew signs that it intended to go
out shortly, and Froggy had yet to put the letter into
the cover, and direct it.

"Do you think, Froggy, the Queen will come
herself?" asked Benny.

"No—I think she'll send p'r'aps one o' the footmans," said Froggy, trying to make the cover stick
with a very grimy little fist pressed down upon it.

"This hanvelope won't stick, Benny—we shall
have to tie it round with a bit o' string. It won't
look so well, but that don't matter."

Of course Froggy had string in his pocket; all
boys have string about them, whatever else they
have not; and from a tangled mass of thick and
fine, Froggy selected the finest piece, and tied the
letter across and across. Then he wrote in large
letters in one corner—"The Queen, Bucknam Palace,"
And then it was all ready for posting.

The little fellows were quite joyful over it, gazing at it, and turning it about with delicious awe, as a thing that would shortly be handled by royalty!

" I can't wait till morning to post it," declared Froggy, putting on his muddy boots which he had taken off. " You go to bed, Benny, and I'll just nip out and do it."

There was no such thing as locking up for the night in Mrs Ragbon's house; the lodgers came and went at any hour they chose; so Froggy was not afraid of being stopped or questioned. He ran out into the silent dark streets, which now only echoed back the steady tramp of a policeman going his rounds, or the hoarse shout of some drunken man or woman beating the air in imaginary conflict with some one. Froggy found a pillar box before long, and into it he slipped the letter, full of a new and burning hope that good would come of it, as he let the flap fall again with a sharp metallic ring. When he got back, he found the narrow little passage stopped up by Mr Blunt, the charwoman's husband, who had come home in a drunken fit, and was calling down vengeance on the head of his hapless wife, who was trembling upstairs in her night dress. He let Froggy pass with an oath, and Froggy mounting the stairs, said to himself, "If ever I marrys a wife, I'll treat her different to that!"

The garret was quite dark now, the rushlight having subsided after a good deal of sputtering and fuss; but Froggy did not mind getting into

bed in the dark, he was so accustomed to it.
Little Benny lay in a deep slumber, dreaming
impossible dreams of splendid scarlet-coated foot-
men appearing in the garret, with messages and
gifts from the Queen, and a new coat for Froggy,
with tails and buttons.

CHAPTER VIII.

THE POLICEMAN'S VISIT.

EARLY the next morning Froggy rose up full of a new plan for obtaining money, which had come into his head during the night. Lying awake, he had heard little Benny beside him, murmuring unconsciously something about "only a little bit o' bread," which showed Froggy that he must be suffering the pangs of hunger in his sleep, and Froggy determined to get him food somehow. He remembered what father had done on one occasion when he was pressed for money to pay for mother's funeral; he went out and pawned some things, and then when he had had some good days out at the West End with the Punch and Judy show, he had called at the pawn-shop again, and redeemed them. Froggy thought he would do the same.

Their stock of worldly goods was very limited, Mrs Ragbon having seized most of them to make up for deficiencies in rent; but there were still a few things remaining, which Froggy could pawn. There was the little mattress on which Froggy

used to lie when he was Benny's age, and an old
waistcoat of father's, and a fur cap, and some shirts
in the old deal box, and something else, wrapped
up very carefully in a cotton handkerchief, which
was very, very sacred, and over which Froggy
sometimes shed a flood of tears. This was mother's
Sunday best bonnet; the one she had always worn,
and which Froggy cried over, because he said, "It
looked so like mother!" It brought back to him
with a vivid recollection her dear face as he remembered it on Sunday evenings in the good old lullaby
days, when Froggy used to say his prayers at her
knee, and tell her all his little troubles. Froggy
wouldn't have pawned this for the world; the coat
off his own back would have to go before he parted
with that, which did the work of the rich boy's
photograph for him. It grieved him to part with
the other things, but he consoled himself with the
thought that it would only, perhaps, be for a few
days. As soon as their letter reached the Queen,
he was confident help would come, and then he
would be able to redeem them.

He told Benny what he was going to do, and
bade him lie quiet in bed till he came back. Then
he tied the things up into a bundle, and crept forth
in the cold, grey morning to seek a shop whose sign
was three golden balls. Trudging along Froggy
made up his mind to go to old Solomons, where
Mac and his wicked companions went yesterday
with their stolen goods. He remembered Dandy

saying he had behaved "like a reg'lar trump," and Froggy thought himself that the old Jew looked like a kind old man, who would be likely to give him the worth of his things.

Not many people were abroad yet ; the dust-carts were going their rounds, and Froggy met some watercress-sellers, and some milkmen, but not many others. There were policemen about, of course, who all seemed to look suspiciously upon Froggy, staggering under the weight of his big bundle. One stopped him at last, and questioned him as to what he had in it, and where he was going.

"Please, sir, h'Im only going to the pawn-shop," said Froggy, opening his bundle with great alacrity for the inquisitive policeman to peep in.

The policeman thrust his hand down, and satisfied himself I suppose, for after a moment he nodded to Froggy, and let him pass on. Then nobody inter-fered with him again, till he reached old Solomon's. Froggy came out of the shop very much delighted, for the pawnbroker gave him more liberal prices than he had ever expected, enough money indeed to last Benny and himself at least six days if they were careful, and at the end of that time, he was sure they would hear from the Queen, if the letter only reached! He was very hopeful, though not quite so sanguine as little Benny, whom he found on his return keeping watch at the garret window, looking for the postman, in case, as he said, 'de letter was already reached, and

de Queen had wrote back quick!' Froggy had laid
some of the money out on his way home. He had
bought some oatmeal and some bread, and a small
supply of charcoal and wood. The little fellows
kindled a fire at once, and put some water on to boil,
and then Froggy made for himself and Benny a nice
large basin of hot porridge, which they shared in
common with a wooden spoon. Froggy said they
would have some "taters" for dinner, and some
more porridge for tea, and altogether they felt quite
rich and comfortable in their poor garret to-day.
Froggy said he shouldn't go crossing-sweeping any
more; he should mend up his jacket, and comb his
hair, and make himself look as "spry" as he could,
and then to-morrow he would try for a place at the
shops as errand-boy.

After their dinner of hot potatoes, Froggy seated
himself, tailor-fashion, on the floor before the fire, and
with a very grave air, began mending his jacket,
which had been torn in the scuffle yesterday. He
was very handy with his needle, and could patch and
darn almost as neatly as a girl, but he made the mistake which most men and boys make when they
work, of taking too long a thread. He sat in his
shirt sleeves with his hair over his eyes and his
lips pouting a little, drawing the needle out over his
shoulder, with such very long threads that each stitch
seemed quite a laborious effort. Benny climbed up to
the sill of the garret window, and there perched himself for the afternoon. He could talk to Froggy from

that position just as well as anywhere else, and he could watch his dear little grey mousie, too, scampering about on the floor picking up the crumbs, and enjoying the new warmth and comfort, which seemed suddenly to have come.

There was a yellow fog rising over London, making everything look hopeless and gloomy outside. The view from the garret window over dingy housetops and blackened chimneys, was dingier and uglier than ever, but Benny seemed not to be happy anywhere away from the window to-day. At every noise in the street, at every new sound that he heard almost, he turned his little white face towards the gloom, and peered out wistfully down into the street below, to see if it were somebody come from the Queen! He quite lost himself in delight now and then picturing what he and Froggy would feel, if a rat-a-tat-tat came at the door, and a scarlet-coated footman did really appear from the Queen, with sacks of coal and beefsteak pies, and money and treacle, and the new-tailed coat for Froggy, and all the other things he had dreamed of in his sleep!

Benny got Froggy by and by to tell him everything about his day yesterday out with Mac. He listened with keen interest to Froggy's description of Chickabiddy and Dandy, with their cunning old men's faces and stunted bodies, and of how they had dodged the policemen, and talked a language of their own, which Froggy knew now was the language of thieves and pickpockets. Froggy was just in the

midst of his story, relating how Mac had robbed the
old gentleman of his pocket-handkerchief, when
suddenly a loud ringing at the street door bell was
heard, and Benny called out excitedly—

" Oh, Froggy, Froggy, I *know* it's the Queen ! "
everybody's lookin' out of dere windows, and the
people in the street are all lookin' up at our house !
It *must* be the Queen, or one of the footmans, Froggy,
or why should they be lookin' ? "

Froggy threw down his jacket, and ran to the window, clambering up, without the aid of a chair, to the
sill beside Benny.

" My ! " cried Froggy, looking out, " there *is* somethink hup, that's sure.   Whatever can it be ? "

The miserable inhabitants of the squalid houses
opposite had thrown open their windows, and were
leaning out into the fog ; some with shawls over their
heads ; some with aprons up to their mouths, and a
few idle-looking men, less careful than the women,
were without their coats, in shirts of a questionable
colour.   On the pavement underneath, and at the
doors and areas, there were more people on the alert,
and swarms of dirty little gutter-children, ragged and
noisy, were taking their share in the popular excitement, whatever it might be.   Quite a buzz of conversation rose from the street, and all the heads and
eyes seemed turned in one direction, and to be centred
upon one spot, namely, the door of Mrs Ragbon's
house !   Froggy got very red in the face, and his
heart beat almost as fast as Benny's, as he craned his

neck, first this way and then that, to get a view down into the street, in high hope, poor little fellow, that if he only stretched his head far enough, he would catch sight of "a grand royal footman," or "a beautifully-dressed gentleman like the West Henders, that would turn out to be one of the Queen's hequerries!"

By and by the sound of angry voices came up from below, and after listening a moment, Froggy and Benny jumped down from the high window-sill, and went out to the stair-head to see what was going on. The house seemed to be in a state of general uproar and commotion. Doors were banging, lodgers were hanging over the banisters, confusion seemed every-where, and above everything, the crying of the children and the noise in the street, was heard Mrs Ragbon's voice ascending from the cellar regions, indignantly protesting against some treatment she deemed "Very 'arsh," and abusing somebody or some persons in no measured terms. Poor Froggy and Benny stared at each other in amazement.

"I don't think it's the Queen *now*, Froggy, do you?" said Benny, looking woefully troubled and disappointed.

"No, that it ain't," said Froggy. "It's a row o' some kind, but I don't know what it's all about."

At that moment, Mrs Blunt, pale and trembling, with her hands all over soapsuds, came out of her room to look over the banisters.

"Please, mum," called Froggy, "can you tell us what's up?"

"Why, it's the perlice come to search the house," called back the charwoman, in a tone of horror. "It's all along o' that good-for-nothing Mac! There's bin a daring jool robbery in the City, and he's in it, and the perlice thinks as how perhaps he brought some o' the watches and things home here, and that we're hidin' of 'em, and they've come to ferrit them out; they've woke little Deb out of such a nice sleep, and she's so ill, poor lamb!"

"Poor Deb," said Benny, "I's so sorry!"

She was Benny's favourite playmate. Then he turned to Froggy with a new and sudden dread, and whispered—

"O Froggy! you don't think the pleece is comin' to take me and you up, cos we knows Mac, does you?"

"No, don't be afeard," said Froggy; "I guess they won't come nigh us. They'll search the kitchens and that, cos they be Mrs Ragbon's places, and she's Mac's mother, but they won't come troublin' no other parties, I reckons."

But Froggy was quite out in his reckoning this time. It soon became evident that the police intended visiting each apartment in its turn, for after they had searched the lower rooms, they mounted to the higher ones, and, armed with the stern majesty of the law, effected their entrance, and commenced stolidly to perform their duty, unmindful of either remonstrance or abuse. Mrs Ragbon followed them on their tour of inspection, and in each case stood at the door, with face all aflame, and arms folded in an attitude of angry resignation, levelling sarcastic remarks and very unparliamentary language at the policeman, while he overhauled her lodger's goods. She was very indignant at the unenviable distinction she would henceforth enjoy amongst her neighbours, from having had her house visited by the police. Ah! if she had been a good mother, and trained up Mac in the way he should have gone, perhaps there would have been none of this sad business.

Up the policeman came nearer and nearer to the garret. In due time he reached the top landing, and went into the charwoman's room, where little sick Deb set up a feeble wail, and the other children a loud cry at the terrible apparition of "a tall live policeman," who they made up their minds at once "had come to take them and mother off to prison!"

"O Froggy! let's come in, and shut the door," said little Benny, pale with fright; "maybe de pleece will think our door's only a cupboard and won't come up!"

"There's nothink to be afeared on—we've not done nothink wrong," said Froggy, getting very red all the same, when the next minute the policeman's heavy tread was heard outside, ascending the ladder staircase step by step, and Mrs Ragbon's angry tones, informing him "he would find nothing but rats and mice up there."

"P'r'aps, missis, its the kind of rats and mice I want

just now," replied the policeman sternly, turning the handle of the door, and breaking in upon the little boys.

Froggy was standing in his shirt sleeves with his face to the door and his hands thrust deep in his pockets, looking rather hot and defiant, as if he were prepared to do battle if he were falsely accused of anything, and little Benny was clinging to him with a white scared face, determined to hang on to Froggy to the very last, and go with him to prison, if the policeman had come to take him.

"Oh, you boys needn't take on—its the way we've *hall* bin treated!" exclaimed Mrs Ragbon angrily, more for the sake of talking at the policeman than from any benevolent idea of calming their fears. "He's paid us hall a visit, quite impartial, because he don't like to make anybody jealous, and now he's come to pay a visit to the rats and mice, wishing to do the civil heverywhere, polite man!"

The policeman took no notice of the landlady, but went straight to the little bed on which Froggy and Benny slept, and began examining it closely.

"Is he goin' to take our bed away, Froggy?" whispered little Benny to Froggy, who was watching the policeman's movements with a sort of scornful anger on his face.

"No, no; I'm not going to take away your bed," said the policeman reassuringly.

"I should think not, indeed!" burst forth Mrs Ragbon again. "Honester boys you wouldn't find than these two—they're as honest as yourself I daresay Mr B 59!"

"Yes, missis, no doubt," returned the policeman, with a slight smile on his grim features.

" I'm sure I don't know which I likes the best—the priests or the perlice," continued the landlady, with a toss of her head; " they both begins with ps, and ones just as great a noosance as t'other, in my opinion. One o' the black-coated gentry comes yesterday a knockin' at the door, disturbin' me and a friend at a winkle tea, but I soon sent him off with some words he won't forget in a hurry!"

Thus did Mrs Ragbon speak of one of those holy men, who spend their lives in knocking at the doors of the poor, with the message of the gospel on their lips, entreating them to listen to the consolations of the Tender Shepherd, in obedience to whose command, ' Feed my lambs,' they come (all honour to them!) in spite of rebuffs and discouragements and rudeness, such as Mrs Ragbon meted out to them. Well may we pray in Dr Monsell's beautiful words—

> " O Saviour! when on life's dark main
> The gospel net seems cast in vain,
> When through the long and cheerless night
> No souls the fishers' toils requite—
> Give them the grace content to be,
> With this one thought—They toil for Thee!"

"Well, now, it's no good making a noise, missis," said the policeman quietly. "I must obey my orders. Your son belongs to a notorious gang of thieves"——

" He do not !" barked Mrs Ragbon.

" Well, p'r'aps we happen to know more about him than you do; at all events, he's wanted now," said Police-constable 59 B; "and my instructions are to search this house from garret to cellar. A bundle was seen to leave your premises this morning, missis, and you are the boy who carried it," he said, turning to Froggy, and eyeing him sharply.

" Yes, sir, I be," answered Froggy, speaking up at once and returning the policeman's glance boldly in the might of conscious innocence. "They was all my things and Benny's, sir. I took 'em to the pawn-shop—old Solomon's in L——— Street."

The policeman jotted down this piece of information in a pocket-book.

" Well, and what was in the bundle?" he asked.

" Well, sir," said Froggy considering, "there was Benny's great coat, and a fur cap of father's, and a mattress as I laid on when I was a young 'un, and a waistcoat and two shirts—that was them."

The policeman asked him a few more questions, the ready answers to which he committed to the pocket-book, and then he turned his attention to the old deal box, where mother's bonnet and Bible were the only things left now.

" Please, sir," said Froggy, as the policeman took it up, "lay hold on that gentle—its mother's bonnet sir, her Sunday best, and she's dead."

" It's rather sensibler than the bonnets they wears now-a-days," remarked the policeman to himself, as he shut down the box again, and rose to his feet.

"Well, now, having discoursed upon the fashions, have you about done?" inquired Mrs Ragbon, in an impudent tone. "P'r'aps as you're such a man for doing your dooty, you had better take a look into the kettle before you leaves."

The policeman appeared not to think this necessary, and having finished his examination of the garret, walked to the door. Just before leaving he turned his head round, and remarked, nodding at Froggy and Benny, "Those boys, missis, look half-starved. They'd be better in 'the House,' I suspects."

"Now, just mind your own business, if you please. I know very well where *you'd* best be, Mr Policeman!" snapped the landlady, as she slammed the door behind her, and followed him downstairs.

The moment the policeman's back was turned, Benny recovered his speech.

"Ah! Froggy," he said, "the policeman didn't know we've wrote to the Queen, when he said that about 'the House,' did he, or he wouldn't a said it. O Froggy! I was just frightened when he come!"

"Was you?" said Froggy.

"Yes, and *you* was a little bit frightened too, now wasn't you, Froggy, just a little at first?" said Benny, trying to coax the admission out of his brother. "Cos your face got so red!"

"Well, I didn't much like it, no more I did,"

replied Froggy, beginning upon his jacket again, and drawing out a very long thread over his shoulder. " Cos I remembered what father used to say—that folks often gets into trouble by going along with other folks that doesn't do right."

" Poor Mac! I'm so sorry he's got into tubble," said Benny. " Do you think he's in prison, Froggy?"

" No, I don't think the p'lice has caught him yet," answered Froggy. " He'll give 'em a lot of trouble. He's so quick and sly."

" Shan't we pray to God not to let Mac be caught?" said Benny.

" Well, I don't know whether that ud be right to pray," answered Froggy, gravely; " God says ' Thou shalt not steal,' and Mac has stole, and God likes people to be punished when they does wrong, or He'd have to punish 'em when they dies!"

" Then we'll pray God to make Mac good, and never to steal no more," said Benny, after a minute. " That'll be better, won't it, Froggy? And we'll ask Jesus to make little Deb well too."

" Yes," said Froggy, " that'll be best."

It was too foggy now to watch at the window any more, and Froggy had finished mending his jacket, so he put the kettle on to boil, and he and Benny had their tea.

CHAPTER IX.

BENNY LOSES HIS PLAYMATES.

EVERAL days passed—cold, miserable, foggy days, in the which Froggy trudged from shop to shop all about great crowded London, trying to get a job, but never getting one, and little Benny kept watch at the garret window with untiring zeal for the scarlet-coated footman who never came. Every day his heart throbbed quicker at the sound of a man's heavy footstep coming up the stair, but every day he was disappointed, for it turned out to be only the parish doctor come to see little Deb Blunt underneath.

The stock of money was getting very low, and things began to look even darker than before, for unless Froggy got a job soon, or they heard from the Queen, they would be without food and fuel again, and this time without anything in the old deal box to pawn. What but starvation or the workhouse stared these poor little boys in the face! Yet their courage never forsook them. Had not God said *that* in the Bible about the little sparrows?

and had not God always taken care of father and mother, and tided them over many bitter troubles, and kept them from the workhouse? They were continually reminding each other of this.

"We dwells very high, you know, Froggy," said Benny once, gazing out of the window over the forest of smoky chimneys, "quite up in the roof, and none of the people in the world seems to 'member you and me's here, but *God* doesn't forget us for that, cos the little sparrows build their nests ever so high in trees and chimleys, and yet God keeps His hi on all of them."

In these days Benny had no one to play with except his mouse. Jack went with older boys, and did not seem to care for playing with Benny any more, and little Deb was too sick to crawl even about the room. Benny missed Deb as a playmate more than he did Jack. When they played at horses she never minded being the horse; when they went to the rubbish heap together, she was always content to hold her pinafore up for Benny to fill, and when a barrel-organ set up in the street, and the little dirty gutter children, God bless them! responded to its music and joined hands and danced, Deb was always Benny's partner. She was a year older than Benny, but because Benny was a boy, she gave up to him in everything, and consequently Benny thought there was no one, in the absence of Froggy, so nice and so desirable as little Deb for a playfellow.

One afternoon Benny got very dull, and longed

for a game at horses with somebody. Froggy was out, and it was raining heavily, and Benny did not think there was a chance that the royal footman would come to-day, because of the rain and the mud; so he gave up watching at the window early, and began thinking about this game of horses. What was he to do for a *horse?* He didn't care for driving a chair; he must have something alive, which would prance and run, and attend to the rein and the whip when he slashed it.

While Benny was busy tying some more knots in his whip and getting the reins ready, he heard the cat "me-yowing" outside, and it occurred to Benny that perhaps Mr Tom was dull like himself this rainy afternoon, and wouldn't mind being his horse just for once. He saw a boy driving a dog in the street, the other day, why shouldn't a cat be driven as well? If Froggy had been at home, he would have told Benny he must not do it, because it would probably teaze the cat. One of the earliest lessons he had learnt from his mother, was one which all little boys and girls should take well to heart, namely, that it is of all things cruel and unkind to do anything that can possibly hurt or teaze dumb animals.

Benny opened the door, and called out in a high tone of encouragement, "Tom! Tom! Tom!" and in walked Tom, looking as sleek and almost as large as a young tiger; a very dangerous enemy indeed for any poor little mouse to meet with out walking. Tom was quite the best-fed inhabitant of the house,

inasmuch as it swarmed with rats and mice, his own
particular food, which no one cared to contest with
him.   Benny knelt down, and began harnessing him,
hissing away as if he were a groom, and saying
gruffly, "Wo, Tommy—wo!   Wo-back, Tommy!"
just as he heard men in the streets addressing their
horses.   Tom was passive under it at first, but the
moment he found that he was getting fettered in
string, and that "*horses*" was to be the game, and he
was to be the horse, he just quietly shook himself
free, turned tail, and scampered down the stairs as
hard as he could.   Ah! the cat who stole the meat
was far too knowing a hand to get caught in such a
one-sided game as that!   Benny was left sitting on
the floor, with the string in his hand, very indignant
and angry at the way in which his steed had given
him the slip.

"You're the nastiest, disagreeablest cat in London!"
cried out Benny as his tail disappeared round the door,
but the cat took no notice and off he scampered.

Left to himself, Benny fell to wondering how long
it would be before little Deb would be able to play at
horses again.   He remembered he had not heard her
cry since daybreak, and the parish doctor hadn't
been to-day, so Benny thought she must be better,
but he was puzzled to know why there was such a
deep, strange hush over the house, and why the
neighbours kept going in and out of Mrs Blunt's
room underneath, softly by turns as if there were
something to see.   Benny got restless and curious,

"You're the nastiest, disagreeablest cat in London!" cried out Benny.

and wished he could see some one to ask how Deb
was. Presently he heard subdued voices on the
landing below, and going out to the stair-head, he
saw Mrs Blunt receiving into her apron a loaf of
bread and some sticks, which a neighbour had been
to fetch for her.

"Mrs Blunt," called out Benny, "how soon'll Deb
be able to play at horses again?"

"O Benny!" answered back the poor mother with
streaming eyes, "you'll never no more have Deb
to play with, nor dance to the organs! She's gone,
Benny—she went this morning, poor lamb, afore ever
any of us was up."

Benny at first only dimly guessed at the meaning
of those words, but gradually as he pondered over
them, the bosom of his little ragged jacket began to
heave up and down, he threw his whip aside, and
covered his eyes with his hands. By this time all his
desire for a game at "horses" had flown away. If
little Deb were dead, then would he not care ever
again to play at horses, or dance to the organs.
"Poor Deb," he kept saying when he thought of her,
"dear little darlin Deb, that I did love so much!"

He sat on the top of the stairs, crying his baby
heart out for some minutes; the rain only keeping
him company as it pattered down drearily on the
glass sky-light above him. Presently Mrs Blunt
came to the foot of the stairs, and said—

"Benny, dear! would you like to see Deb in her
coffin?"

Benny sobbed "Yes," and with a tiny fist in each eye began slowly to descend step by step, till he reached Mrs Blunt, who took him up in her arms as if he were a very light weight, and carried him into her one poor room, where the dead child lay. The room was profoundly still, though it was full of people. There were all Deb's brothers and sisters, huddled up together and speaking in whispers, as if something very strange and terrible had happened. There was Mr Blunt sitting over the handful of fire, with an empty gin bottle at his elbow, in a state of maudlin sorrow; and there were two or three poorly-clad, dejected-looking women in one corner, gazing intently upon the small body which lay in its coffin, unspeakably still and waxen white, ready for burial the next morning. How calm and peaceful little Deb looked!—all the suffering gone out of her old woman's face, all her cries hushed, all the wrinkles smoothed away, as if for her

> " Morning's joy had ended the night of weeping,
>   And life's long shadows had broken in cloudless love ! "

Happy little Deb! who need have wept for her? Yet the poor mother wept sorely afresh as she stood, with Benny in her arms, beside the coffin.

"Oh, my dear, I wouldn't fret about it overmuch if I was you," said one poor woman, who looked as if she had found the waves of this world very trouble-some. " Life's a sad business, take it altogether from cradle to grave, and its worse I ses for women than for men. We don't likes to lose 'em when we've got 'em; no

more we does, bless their innocent hearts, but depend
upon it children's best out of it all ! "

"Yes, that they be," said an older neighbour mournfully. "Robert and me, we've had seven, and we've
buried 'em all, and we thank the Lord for it now,
though we grieved terrible at first ! "

" I shall have to go to work after to-morrow," said
the bereaved mother, who would not have called her
child back again if she could ; she loved it too well
for that ! "But I must have my cry to-day," she
sobbed.

"Yes—yes, my dear, have your cry to-day," said
the neighbours kindly. " It'll do her good, poor
thing ! "

While the women were talking Benny was gazing
wonderingly upon little Deb, and pondering deeply
in his baby fashion over the mysterious change which
had come, but not shedding many tears. He was
thinking of a hymn Froggy had taught him to say
on Sundays—

> " Tender Shepherd, Thou hast stilled
> Now Thy little lamb's brief weeping ;
> Ah, how peaceful, pale, and mild,
> In its narrow bed 'tis sleeping ;
> And no sigh of anguish sore
> Heaves that little bosom more ! "

" I sha'n't cry any more, I don't think," whispered
Benny at length to Mrs Blunt, drying up the last
tear with an end of his tattered jacket, and giving his
nose a doleful rub ; then laying his little dirty white

cheek lovingly against her's, he whispered his sweet conviction, "Cos Deb's gone to Jesus, I's sure, that's why, and she's hearin' music more beautifuller than the organs, and will nebber be cold or have pains again!"

He leant over the coffin and kissed Deb's small, still face, saying hushfully, "O Debbie! goodbye!—goodbye, Debbie!"

Then there was a knock at the door, and some more neighbours came softly in to look at the dead child, and Mrs Blunt gave Benny a crust and told him to go upstairs again.

What do you think had happened in the garret during Benny's absence? Something that almost broke his heart, poor little fellow. He had left the door open, the cat had stolen up, and killed his mouse! Yes, there it lay on the floor, in the midst of the crumbs it had been nibbling, when the treacherous cat had pounced upon it from the back, with its small grey limbs stretched out, its eyes shut, and its tail quite cold and lifeless.

At first Benny would not believe it was dead—he called to it, he stroked it, he kissed it; he called to it again in the frantic hope that it was only asleep; but when at last he found that it responded neither to sound nor caress, but lay cold and dull and limp (so unlike his mousie that used to be so bright and nimble!) Benny threw himself on the floor beside it, and gave himself up to a passion of grief. He was lying there still and crying bitterly when Froggy came home an hour later.

"Why, Benny, Benny darlin', whatever is the matter?" cried out Froggy.

"I've lost my mouse," sobbed Benny. "Oh, I did love that 'ittle mouse so!" regarding his slain pet with the most pitiful streaming eyes.

Froggy looked as if he could have cried too. He came, full of concern, and knelt down beside the mouse, and gently laid his finger for one moment on its little heart, which had ceased to beat some time.

"Yes," said Froggy, with the air of a grave physician, "he be dead, Benny, so he be. Whatever killed him?"

"The cat," sobbed Benny. "I left the—door open when—I went down to see—Deb in her coffin, Froggy, to say goodbye—and he come up, and he did it! And he'd a eat it, too, in another minute if I hadn't come up!"

"Is Deb dead?" asked Froggy, with a blank look of sorrow on his face. "Poor Debbie! When did she die?"

"Dis mornin'," sobbed Benny, "when we was all asleep;" then turning his pitiful eyes towards Froggy he said mournfully, "Everythink seems to die, Froggy —why is it?"

"Cos it's good, I spects," answered Froggy, after he had pondered a moment.

"Why good?" asked Benny.

"Cos it comes from Jesus," said Froggy. "The nurse as was in the 'ospital, time father and me was took there, said as we was always to try and think

everythink Jesus did was good, whether He took
away things ever so; then He'd never leave us, she
said, not never. I often thinks on her words, I do,
and I does try."

Benny waited a moment as if he were thinking
over what Froggy had said, then he looked up, and
asked—

"'Posin *I* was to die, Froggy, like little Deb and
mouse, would you say to Jesus that was good too?"

The question seemed to startle Froggy and greatly
to distress him. He gazed at his brother for one
moment with a great look of pain, then a flood of
tears came, and throwing his arms round Benny's
thin, white neck, he hugged him tightly to him, and
cried vehemently—

"Oh no, no, no, Benny, I don't think as ever I
could say it was good if Jesus was to take *you* away.
Don't never talk of dying again, Benny. If you was
to die I would die. O Benny, Benny! however could
I live here alone?"

"It wouldn't be such a bad thing if God 'ud take
us both," said Benny; "but I wouldn't never like to
go such a long journey all alone by myself without
you, Froggy; oh, no!" and he tried to kiss his
brother's tears away. "I's not so sorry about little
Deb as mouse, Froggy; cos I shall meet Deb again
in heaven, if I'm a good little boy, and gets there,
but I shan't never meet my mouse any more."

"I'll get you another mouse, Benny," said Froggy,
yearning to comfort him.

"I couldn't ever love another," said Benny, nodding his head dolefully. "There'll never be a mouse *quite* like him again, Froggy. Oh, to think of his bright, merry eyes being shut, and that he'll *never* go into his little hole again!"

This last seemed a heart-breaking reflection. He sobbed afresh, and poor Froggy could in nowise console him.

Benny went to bed quite a heartbroken little boy this evening. He had his dead mouse laid somewhere where he could see it, and he put a little crumb of bread by it the last thing, in the forlorn hope that it might come to life again in the night, and eat it.

CHAPTER X.

FROGGY CALLS AT BUCKINGHAM PALACE.

THE next morning a tall, cadaverous-looking man, with a pale face and very black whiskers, who Froggy knew was an undertaker, came and carried little Deb away in her coffin. A sad procession started from the back-room, and stumbled down the steep stairs. The poor mother, as chief mourner, followed first, dressed in the black clothes which kind neighbours had lent her for the occasion; then followed all Deb's brothers and sisters, and lastly came Robert's wife, the poor woman who said she had buried seven children, and thanked the Lord for it now! She was going to follow with Mrs Blunt to the cemetery.

As the mournful party passed out at the door, a barrel organ in the street struck up a lively Scotch reel, the very tune to which the dead child being now borne along in her coffin had so often danced with Benny. Froggy and Benny were both at the window, peering down into the street with eager, sorrowful eyes, to catch a glimpse of the funeral.

"O Froggy, Froggy!" cried Benny, bursting into tears, "why does the organ play that, Froggy? It seems to be callin' to her to dance!"

"Don't never cry like that, Benny," entreated Froggy, with his arms about Benny in a moment. "Don't listen to it; it's a hugly organ." Then in a cheerful tone, he said, "Shall I tell you, now, what you and me'll do when winter's gone, and summer's come, and the evenin's is beautiful and light, Benny?"

"Yes," said Benny, nodding his head.

"Well, we'll go to the cimentery, you and me, and we'll visit little Deb's grave," said Froggy, "father and me went once to visit mother's, and oh! it was such a nice place. The birds was singin', and there was trees, and father said it was somethink like country."

"Tell me more about dat place," said Benny.

"There was buttercups and daisies growin'," said Froggy. "The rich people takes flowers and plants them on the graves, but poor people what can't afford flowers picks the buttercups and daisies, and lays 'em on. That's what you and me'll do, Benny; we'll pick a beautiful bunch, and lay it on Deb's grave."

The thought of this summer's evening visit to the cemetery seemed to comfort and soothe Benny, and he dwelt much upon it.

Benny's mouse had not come to life again during the night, and Froggy told Benny they must think about burying it somehow. At first Benny said he

couldn't let it be buried, and begged Froggy not to
talk about it, but when Froggy said that if Mrs
Ragbon came up and saw it, she would very likely
throw it into the dust-hole or give it to the cat,
Benny changed his mind, and became instantly
anxious that his mouse should be given decent and
honourable burial. So they wrapped its little dead
body up in a winding-sheet of rag, and laid it in a
coffin, which Froggy made out of an old rushlight
box. Then they sallied forth with it to the piece
of waste ground, where there was that rubbish-heap,
to which Benny had so often gone with Deb, and
which seemed such an everlasting joy to the children
of the neighbourhood.

I am sure that these poor East End children
fancied themselves on a kind of " Tom Tiddler's
ground," picking up gold and silver! while they
burrowed about amongst the oyster-shells and rubbish, filling their pinafores and baskets with the
treasures that turned up. It is true that not many
things had come to the surface as yet more valuable
than old boots, crazy tea-kettles, dead cats, and bat-
tered straw bonnets without their crowns, but then
there was always the delightful feeling that at any
moment, something more valuable *might* turn up!
Their mothers had told them wonderful stories of
golden sovereigns and diamond rings being sometimes found at the bottom of rubbish-heaps, and
these stories had got repeated from lip to lip
amongst the noisy, clamorous children, and had

fired them with such hope, that they never seemed to tire of their digging and delving and burrowing. Ah! what an angel friend is Hope! How would the digging and delving and burrowing of this life be got through with, I wonder, without her!

Froggy and Benny went to the quietest corner of the waste ground, and there buried the mouse. Froggy took Benny by the hand coming home, and prattled away to him to cheer him up, for he observed that his little brother was very sad, and that the tears kept rolling down his white cheeks, though he tried to hide them, and to answer back cheerfully when Froggy spoke to him.

The next few days passed much like other days, only that Benny seemed to be quieter after the death of his playmates, and not to take quite the same interest in things that he used to do. He still spent much of his time at the garret window, but it was no longer to watch for the Royal footman. He went there now to gaze up at the foggy sky, and to speculate upon the Beautiful City that lies beyond, whither "gentle Jesus" had carried little Deb, and where she was now "hearing music more beautifuller than the organs!" Froggy continued to trudge about London in search of a place, each day setting out with more energy, and walking farther afield, as each day the money became less, and he saw little Benny's cheeks growing paler. Wherever he saw a card in the shop-windows saying "Boy wanted," in he turned, and besought anxiously

I

the master or mistress to take him ; but none of
them would do so. Some said he was too small;
some said they were suited, others that he was too
weak or too young, and a great many bade him
roughly be off out of their shop at once, as
they didn't want a ragged dirty little rascal like
him ! Poor Froggy—how hurt and red he looked
sometimes, when these unkind answers were given
him ! At last, when there was but one shilling left
of the pawnbroker's money, and nearly eight days
had gone by without any answer coming from the
Queen to their letter, Froggy said to Benny—

" I knows what I shall do, Benny; I'll go to
Buck'nam Palace, and ask if the Queen ever got
our letter, I will. Maybe she's not wrote, cos she's
at Windsor Castle, or up in that country top of
h'England, that mother used to tell me about, where
the folks eats oat-cakes, and plays the bagpipes, and
the swell gents at the West End wears peddicoats,
and goes to shoot birds, when town's hempty."

Having made up his mind, Froggy started directly
after he had had his breakfast; for Buckingham
Palace, he knew, was a long way off, though he did
not know the road to it quite. He remembered
seeing the Palace once, a long time ago, from St
James' Park, when he and his mother and father had
crossed it, late one winter's afternoon on their way
home, and they stopped awhile by the water to watch
the merry, muffled-up skaters on the ice, and Froggy
went on with father, and had a nice little slide like all

the other boys who were there. Froggy knew there would be no skaters to-day, for the weather was not quite frosty enough for ice, though there was a bitter wind abroad, and as soon as he got out of the poor Shoreditch neighbourhood, he met gentlemen, muffled up in warm winter coats, and ladies in sealskins and furs, just as he saw them when there was snow on the ground. Froggy shivered along, with his shoulders up to his ears, and a hand in each sleeve, trying to keep the cruel wind from cutting down his poor little neck at the back, and from stealing up his arms in front. He had no warm flannel jersey and drawers on like most of the little boys he met trotting along by the side of their mammas; Froggy's clothing was of the thinnest and scantiest, and it was impossible to keep the cold out.

Early in the day's journey he inquired of a policeman whether he was going right for Buckingham Palace, and the policeman, bending low down to listen to him, answered very good-naturedly—

"Oh yes, you're all right for it, though you are not near it yet, you have still a goodish step to go;" then he directed Froggy as well as he could, though Froggy was yet so far from the Palace, he found it extremely difficult to follow the policeman in all his directions about turning first to the right, and then to the left, and then to the right again, and so on. By the time he had done waving his long arm about, Froggy was staring up at him in a state of hopeless bewilderment, having failed to take in anything.

The policeman perceiving this, finished up by saying—

"Well, I tell you what it is, little chap—you see
that timber cart there; follow that as long as it keeps
straight ahead, and then ask your way again."

Froggy trotted briskly off, having thanked the
policeman, and walked along by the side of the
timber cart for some time. By and by his feet grew
very weary, and he thought how nice it would be to
get a ride on the timber, which was high in the air in
front, but low down, almost touching the road at the
back. The carter would perhaps never turn round,
and if he did, thought Froggy, well, he could jump off
quick, before he had time to give him a cut with his
whip. So Froggy ran out into the muddy road, and
giving a slight jump backwards perched himself safely
on the end of a plank, which was waving gently up
and down with the motion of the sturdy horses in
front. It made Froggy quite an easy, springy seat,
and he rode along in high contentment for a mile or
two. He only wished Benny was beside him, having
a ride too! Presently, like most good things, it came
to an end, for some boys passing, shouted out to the
carter, "Put the whip behind! Put the whip behind!"
and the man, suddenly rousing himself, and becoming
aware of the two little strange legs dangling from the
plank at the back, began lashing his whip round;
but not in time to catch Froggy. On the first alarm,
he jumped nimbly to the ground, and was on the
pavement again before the whip could touch him.

This little ride had helped him on his way nicely, and enabled him to walk out bravely afterwards. He constantly asked policemen and cabmen if he were going right for the Palace, and they all assisted him, in pointing out the way, and setting him right when he was wrong. At length, after much weariness, and rather late in the day, Froggy found himself on the broad open road, outside the gates of Buckingham Palace, which looked very grand and vast, with its long rows of windows and stone figures on the outside, and large inner entrance embellished with the Royal monogram in gold. Froggy looked up at it with great awe, and wondered whether it were possible that his and Benny's letter, written in the poor garret in Shoreditch, could have passed through those splendid gates into the presence of the Queen! His heart sank a little when he remarked that there was no flag flying from the Royal roof, and that the windows were all closed like the windows of the houses in the West End when London was empty; Froggy thought the Queen could not be there! He resolved, however, to ask, and he began looking about the majestic iron gates for a bell, or a knocker, but he could not see one anywhere. There was a sentry box close by, and a tall soldier was on duty keeping guard over the Palace, taking rather brisk turns backwards and forwards to his box, as the weather was so cold. It required some courage to do so, but Froggy made up his mind, as his business was so important, to ask this tall soldier where the bell was.

Accordingly Froggy approached him, and looking up into his face, said softly—

"If you please, sir"——

But the soldier continued his march, with his chin up in the air, and his eyes well to the front, as if he never saw Froggy. He was so accustomed to being stared at and admired by little boys like Froggy, that not having heard him speak, he took no particular notice of him, and passed on. "P'r'aps as he's milingtary, he don't like being called *sir*," thought Froggy. "I'll try somethink else"—and he planted himself straight before the soldier, and addressed him again by a new title—

"If you please, captain," he said, "can you tell me where the bell is?"

The soldier pulled himself up short now, and glanced down over his stiff collar at the small red-nosed urchin beneath him. If Froggy's face had not been so grave and anxious, the soldier would have thought he was quizzing him, for the soldier's rank in the British army was not that of captain, or anything like it.

"The bell?" he repeated. "What bell do you mean?"

"Why, the bell as people rings that wants to go into the Palace, captain," said Froggy. "I wants to send a message into the Queen, by one o' the footmans."

"Her Majesty's at Windsor," said the soldier, with a little smile which Froggy did not see, as he was so

"I wants to send a Message in to the Queen," said Froggy.

Page 134.

very low down. "What is your message?" he asked, as Froggy looked very crest-fallen and sad.

"Why, it's just this," said Froggy, "it's to ask if she ever got the letter as two little chaps wrote her from Shoreditch, eight days ago. She'd remember it, she would, cos it was a letter tied up with string, tellin' her all about theirselves, and how poor we was, and everythink. We think she can't never a got it, or she'd a wrote back afore this, and I've come over just to see."

"The letter hasn't reached, I suspects," said the soldier kindly. "You had better try again—p'r'aps you'll have better luck next time."

He commenced walking up and down again, for it was cold standing, and poor little Froggy, with a weight of disappointment at his heart, crossed over into St James' Park, where he perched himself on the edge of a seat, and began shedding a few quiet tears.

There were not many people in the Park; those who were seemed principally to be making short cuts across it from one gate to another, with parcels in their hands, and business in their faces. They were all too intent upon their own affairs, to cast a thought on poor miserable little Froggy, who sat there in the damp and gloom, till the lights on Constitution Hill and in Piccadilly began to twinkle and glimmer through the leafless trees. Then Froggy, frozen almost into an icicle, took to his feet again, and began his homeward journey, choosing the line of streets where there appeared to be the most gas, and traffic, and

warmth. How he envied those people whom he saw
eating hot chestnuts, and drinking hot coffee at the
stalls! Presently he saw a great crowd in the distance, and he hurried forward with a boy's irresistible
curiosity to join it, and see what was going on.
Perhaps it was a fight, or a cab accident, or a show
of some kind; at any rate, it must be something
interesting, he thought, to attract such a crowd. As
he got nearer he could see that it was assembled
round and about a large public-house, which stood
commandingly at the corner of a street where two
busy thoroughfares met. The gas was flaring con-
spicuously from showy burners and glass chandeliers
inside, and through the windows there streamed
enough light to light up every face in the crowd. The
people in the road were pushing and jostling one
another to get nearer the pavement, and those on the
pavement were pressing close up against the public-
house door, as though they were expecting it to open
shortly, and that then something exciting would
issue forth, which would be all the better seen from
a front place.

"What's the row, matey?" asked Froggy of a
newspaper boy who was wedging himself in, on the
outskirts of the crowd.

"Why, the p'leece has gone in there to fetch out a
chap as they've bin wanting ever so long," returned
the newspaper boy with a chuckle; "and there's no
hend of a row. 'E's tryin' to hide, they ses, though
there's two p'leece."

"What's the chap bin doing?" asked Froggy.

"Why, he's the one as throwed the snuff in the City jool robbery last week," answered the boy, as if he expected Froggy to know all about the audacious young thief, who had thrown snuff in the jeweller's face to disable him while his confederates sacked the shop.

At the mention of the jewel robbery, Froggy pricked up his ears; for the recollection of the policeman's visit to Mrs Ragbon's house came suddenly into his head, together with those words of the charwoman: "It's all along o' that good-for-nothing Mac! There's bin a darin' jool robbery in the City, and he's in it"—etc., etc.

"What if it should be Mac?" thought Froggy, and his heart began to beat with a strange and painful excitement. He knew there was no chance of seeing from where he was, for everybody towered high above him, and he was too small to force his way into the crowd, like the newspaper boy, who was taller. So he determined to climb a lamp-post that was near.

He got a man standing by to give him a "leg up;" then he worked himself to the top with the agility of a young monkey, and clung there, looking right over the heads of the people, and able from his superior height to get a better view of the public-house door than any one. At last the moment of excitement came; there was a great noise and movement amongst the crowd; the great swinging doors of the public-house burst open suddenly; a flood of light streamed

forth, and two policemen appeared, holding on sternly
to something that was kicking and ducking and struggling, and being dragged along between them. At
first Froggy could not see who it was they had got,
whether it was a boy or a man ; but when in another
minute they turned sharply to the right and passed
close under the lamp-post, followed by the murmuring
tramping rabble which always accompanies a prisoner
to the station-house in London, Froggy caught his
breath, and uttered a sharp cry of dismay, for the gaslight showed beyond all doubt that it was none other
than the landlady's son, Mac Ragbon! It was a
terrible sight to see. He had no hat on, his hair was
rough, and his face was ghastly pale with marks of
blood on it ; his shirt was torn, and his jacket was
being carried by one of the policemen. Evidently
he had been resisting his capture to the last.

Froggy slid soberly down from the lamp-post after
they had passed, and regained his feet with a heavy
sigh. "That's what comes of leading a bad life and
thieving," thought he, looking very grave and de-
pressed by what he had seen. "I sha'n't tell Benny
nothink about it, I don't think, cos he's so down now,
poor little chap, about Deb and his mouse. And he'd
fret ever so about Mac, if I was to tell him he's gone
to prison!"

At this moment a gentleman's brougham piled up
with luggage, on its way to the Great Eastern Railway
station, passed slowly through the crowd, and Froggy's
quick eye perceived that there was a place at the back,

on which he could seat himself for a ride ! He jumped on, and had a long undisturbed lift homewards, for the course of the carriage was (luckily for Froggy) exactly his, and passed the very end of the street where he lived.

CHAPTER XI.

BENNY HAS "THE STAGGERS."

ROGGY never forgot his coming home this evening. In after years it was as indelibly impressed upon his mind, as that other coming home long ago on the bleak December night, when mother was taken "fainty-like in the passage, and couldn't get upstairs nohow!"

Benny was generally on the top stair waiting to greet Froggy on his return home, but he was not there to-night. Benny generally lit a light in the garret, to make it look warm and cheerful for him when he came home, but there was no light burning to welcome Froggy to-night; everything seemed strangely dark and silent, and when Froggy called out "Benny!" and again "Benny!" no answer came. Froggy, much puzzled, groped his way up the stairs. As he did so, the thought struck him that perhaps Benny was playing him a trick, and was going to jump out upon him suddenly, so he paused on the threshold of the garret, and said, "I say, Benny, where be you? Come out, Benny!" No answer. "I knows where you be,

Benny, you're behind the door," said Froggy, getting rather uneasy, and advancing a few·steps in order to bring matters to an issue, if Benny really were hiding. Froggy waited anxiously for a moment. At first he could only hear the sound of his own breathing, but presently a little sigh caught his ear, and a slight movement coming from the direction of the bed.

"Benny, do speak!" cried Froggy. "Where be you?"

"I's here," said a very faint small voice from the darkness.

At that moment a great black cloud, which had hitherto obscured the moon, drifted right away from her, and a long beautiful silver moonbeam came slanting in through the window, lighting up the whole of the garret, and falling full upon what looked like a desolate little heap of corduroy lying on the floor between the window and the bed. Froggy started forward, for it was Benny.

"Benny! Benny! what's the matter? ain't you well?" he said with a great cry in his voice.

"I's not very," said Benny, trying to rise.

The moonlight fell on his face, and such a poor little face it was! white and drawn, and without an atom of colour on the lips.

"Do you feel fainty-like? What is it you feels, darlin'?" questioned Froggy with a terrible look of anxiety in his face, as he pressed it close up into Benny's.

"I think I's got what the cab-horses has," said

Benny, staring at Froggy as he stood with great haggard eyes. " I's got the staggers, Froggy !" and as he spoke, his little legs, which were trembling and knocking together beneath him, gave way, and he fell to the ground.

" Oh dear ! oh dear ! oh dear ! " moaned Froggy aloud in the extremity of that deep loneliness which the strongest of us have all felt at times, when sudden danger has overtaken us, and there has been none to help.

But he was only dismayed for a moment. Was not God above, watching over them still ? His lips did not move, but his heart went up instantly to God in the short ejaculatory prayer—" O God, I'm quite alone ; teach me what to do ! " The moment he had said it, he felt stronger to act, because he was sure God would guide him. Mother had always prayed in times of sickness and peril, and God had never failed mother ; she had always said that, even through the darkest times, and the remembrance of this greatly comforted and strengthened Froggy.

O mothers and fathers ! how your words and examples come back to your children, and influence them either for good or for evil, long after the grave has closed over you, and you are alike powerless to impress deeper that which is good or to recall that which is evil.

Froggy gathered his wits together, and lit a candle. Then he lifted Benny in his arms, and carrying him to the bed began to undress him ; much as he had undressed him years ago, on the sad December night when mother was so ill, and father had told him to put Benny to bed, because mother would not be able to do it. Benny was a baby then and slept on the Punch and Judy box, now he was six years old and slept on the mattress; but it seemed to Froggy that his little brother was quite as feeble and helpless and dependent to-night as ever he had been then; Benny lay very still with his eyes closed, across Froggy's small lap, now and then sobbing, but not shedding any tears.

"Cheer up, darlin'!" Froggy kept saying softly, while he took one thing off, and then another in nervous haste. "I knows all about it, I do, and I'll soon get you better. I knows of a medicine that I'm agoin' to buy, Benny, that'll warm you ever so, and make you better. Mother always gave it father and me when we was ill, always."

This last was added by way of comfort to himself; for anything mother used to do, Froggy thought, must be right to do in any case.

When Benny was undressed, Froggy laid him on the mattress, and with great care and anxiety tucked the scanty clothing well in about him to keep him warm.

"I'm going to the chemist's now, darlin'," whispered Froggy leaning over him. "I sha'n't be away not two minutes, I'll be back afore ever you can count three, Benny!"

He kissed his little brother's white face, as if he

were loth to leave him even for two minutes; then he took the last remaining shilling of the pawnbroker's money (the only money he had in the world!), and ran out into the streets to find a chemist's shop. The tears streamed down his cheeks as he fled along. "O God, make Benny better," he kept praying. "Pray God, make Benny better!"

He had not to go far; at the end of the next street he discovered a chemist's shop, and into it he ran breathlessly, and inquired of the man if he kept "Keating's Lixy?"

"Keating's Elixir?—oh yes, we keep it; there you are, sevenpence-halfpenny to pay," said the chemist, handing him over the counter a tall, narrow bottle with a seal at the top, and a very large label upon it.

Froggy grasped it eagerly as the thing that was to make Benny well; then, having paid for it, he ran out again into the streets to go home. But it suddenly struck him that there was no food for Benny in the house, and no fuel either, except one or two knobs of charcoal. He had still fourpence-halfpenny left; this, he reflected, would buy some oatmeal and a bundle of sticks to make a fire. He ran to an open green-grocer's shop a few doors farther down, where the gas was flaring lavishly amongst cabbages and vegetables, and great sacks of potatoes. The man who kept the shop dealt in other commodities besides, and here Froggy was able to buy both the oatmeal and the sticks. For these things he gave

his last penny in payment, scarcely realising it was
his last, and then home he hurried as fast as he could
fly.

On entering the garret he ran to the mattress
the first thing, to have a look at Benny. He was
lying just as he had left him, apparently not having
moved, but his teeth were chattering now, and he
looked whiter than before. He did not speak, but
he opened his eyes, and looked pitifully at Froggy
for one moment, as if he were appealing to him, like
some poor little dumb animal, for help.

"Yes, Benny! I knows all about it," responded
Froggy soothingly. "You're agoin' to be warmed
d'rectly, Benny, and have some beautiful, comfortin'
medicine that I've bin and bought."

He left the bedside, and set to work energetically
to light the fire. This was no easy task to accom-
plish, for a keen blast of wind came pouring down
the chimney, and kept continually putting it out
at first. It was some time before Froggy could get
a nice bright blaze to start up, but the moment this
occurred he pulled off the little jacket from his own
back, and kneeling down in his shirt-sleeves, began
holding it close to the bars, as if he were desirous
of making it into toast. He held the jacket there
till it was thoroughly warmed through and through,
then he jumped up and ran with it in eager haste
to the mattress, and wrapped it about Benny.

"There, darlin'! isn't that nice? Isn't that
splendid?" he said, tucking it in at all corners;

K

"and when it gets cold, I'll warm it again. Don't speak afore you're able, Benny, but just tell me when you're beginning to get a bit warmer, will you ? " whispered poor anxious Froggy, who was longing to hear Benny speak again.

Froggy hurried off now, and began busying himself about the medicine. There was the seal to be broken, and the cork of the bottle to be drawn, and water to be boiled, because mother, he remembered, always mixed it in warm water, and of course he must do the same. Before long a small, muffled voice came from the bed, " I's warmer, Froggy," it said.

Benny was certain to say he was better the. first moment he could ; he was such a gallant-hearted little fellow by nature, and always made the best of things. When he was a baby, and fell down and hurt himself, he used to call out, " Up again ! " and up he would jump at his own word of command, with a merry laugh to hide the tears if there were any. This was fortunate, since he had never had a mother to run to him,

> " And kiss the place
> To make it well."

"Oh, I be so glad ! " cried Froggy. "I'll warm the jacket agin, as soon as ever you've took the medicine, Benny. 'Ere it be, nice and hot ! " He spoke in a brisk tone, and came running with it to the bedside.

" Is it good for ' staggers ' ? " inquired Benny, from under the jacket.

He had nestled so low down, that nothing could be seen of him now except his forehead, and a little bit of his turned-up nose. " Oh yes, it's good for *heverythink !* " replied Froggy warmly, stirring it round energetically with a spoon. " Mother said it ud cure colds, coughs, nooralgy, tic, 'eadache, hearache, toothache, and every other kind of hache that you can think of ! "

Benny tried to rise, but Froggy had to lift him up and hold the cup to his lips. At the sight of the nauseous brown liquid, Benny shuddered and drew back.

" Why, darlin' ! it ain't near so bad as castor oil, nor grey powder," said Froggy encouragingly, giving it another stir.

" It's badder," said Benny ruefully, returning to it, however, and putting his lips to it again. But a second time he drew back.

" Come ! it's all getting cold," said Froggy, stirring it with renewed vigour. " Now, be a good boy, and take it, there's a darlin' ! "

Benny regarded it for a moment as if he were trying to make up his mind, then he said pleadingly —" Take a little drop first, Froggy ! "

" Well, I will—I don't mind it a bit," said Froggy and he took a taste.

" You made a face after it ! " said Benny, nodding.

" Yes, that was cos I sipped it," explained Froggy

" It wouldn't be near so bad in a draught. Now, I'll count one, two, three, and when I says *three*, Benny, you must take it. I always took it when mother said three."

Then he counted slowly " one—two—*three!*" At " three," Benny brought his trembling lips to the medicine very slowly and cautiously, Froggy gave the cup a little tip up, and Benny was obliged to swallow a sip. But he took no more. He turned his face away from it shudderingly again, and some of it got spilt on the bedclothes.

Froggy was in despair ; he felt overcome with the weight of his responsibilities to-night, and what should he do if he could not get Benny to take the medicine ? Benny must be very ill, he was sure, to look as he did, so dreadfully white and haggard, and there was no time for dilly-dallying ! Froggy determined to try what scolding would do, since persuasion had no effect.

" You're a naughty boy, Benny," he said at last.

" I'm not a naughty boy," said Benny in a very doleful voice, laying his head back on the pillow.

" Yes, you is, or you'd take your medicine," said Froggy ; " you ain't being a good boy at all, going on like this ! Whatever would Jack say if he was to know ? "

Benny did not answer, and Froggy waited a moment. Then he tried something else.

" Deb always took *her* medicine," he said.

Ah ! this evidently had made an impression.

Benny's large eyes turned attentively towards Froggy, and he regarded him steadily for a moment, as if he were thinking over his words.

"She knew Jesus wouldn't love her if she didn't," continued Froggy. "And she used to bear her mustard poultices, too, like a brick."

"Did she?" said Benny ponderingly; then suddenly, "I'll be a brick, too, Froggy!" he exclaimed, and to Froggy's astonishment he raised his little, frail body in bed, took the cup between his hands, and drained it to the very dregs.

"Yes, you was a brick, then!" said Froggy admiringly, looking into the cup to see if he had left any, and finding none. "It wasn't so bad as you thought, now, was it, darlin'?"

"Worser," said Benny, giving a great heave, and the tears coming into his eyes with the effort of keeping the medicine where it ought to be after swallowing it.

"I'll get you a nice basin of oatmeal, now," said Froggy. "It'll take the taste out beautiful."

"I couldn't eat none," said Benny, nodding his head.

"Well, I don't know as I'll press you to it," said Froggy thoughtfully; "cos I don't think mother give me supper when I took the Lixy. But I'll warm up the jacket agin!"

He carried it to the fire, and held it to the bars as before. While he was busy down on his knees, turning the jacket first this way and then that, he heard

Benny murmur "I's so hot!" and give a little sigh. Froggy turned his head round quickly, and saw that Benny was now lying with his arms out of bed, and the clothing below his chest, as if it were a hot summer's night.

"There! wasn't I right? Ain't it a lovely medicine for warmin?" cried Froggy with enthusiasm, running to the bedside to rejoice over his patient. "Mother always said it—there wasn't nothink like it in the world."

But when Froggy came to look at Benny, he was not quite so satisfied. Benny was looking very odd and unlike himself. Froggy took up one of his little hands to feel, and it was burning hot to his touch.

"Do you feels all right, darlin'?" asked Froggy, peering anxiously into his face.

"Yes, only I got a neadache," said Benny, turning his head restlessly about on the pillow, "and I are so hot, I'd like to kick everythink off me, I would!"

"Oh, you mustn't never do that!" exclaimed Froggy gravely. "You'd catch your death o' cold."

"Froggy," said Benny staring at him, "'as my 'ead growed very big?"

"Why, no, it ain't no bigger than it was," replied Froggy, examining it carefully. "Do it feel big?"

"Yes," said Benny, "I feels just like the picters the men wheels about of the hobgobblins in the pantomimes, with little funny bodies, and large big heads!"

At that moment, a small bare leg made its appearance out at the side of the bed.

" Benny, take your leg in," said Froggy, covering it up, "the medicine won't do you not a scrap of good if you tosses about like that ! When I used to take the Lixy mother always made me cover up after it, and keep warm, and get into a nice sleep if I could. Don't you think if you was to try now, darlin,' you might get to sleep ? "

Benny agreed to try. "But I must say my prayers first, and ' Gentle Jesus,' " he said.

" Oh yes ! of course, and I'll come and sit by you while you ses 'em," said Froggy, perching himself on the side of the mattress, and looking very affectionately at his little sick brother, who now folded his hands in preparation for saying those simple prayers, that he had been in the habit of saying so regularly and easily every morning and evening since babyhood.

But, oh, what did ail Benny to-night ? He seemed not to be able to say them. After the first few words, " Pray God bless"—his speech became confused, his words ran in to each other, and it all sounded like gibberish. He seemed to know, poor little fellow ! that he was doing something wrong, for his countenance became distressed, and at last he stopped and gazed helplessly at Froggy, as much as to say, "O Froggy, tell me what is the matter with me ? " with that irresistibly touching look in his eyes that we see sometimes in the eyes of dumb animals when they are in pain, and which is quite as eloquent as speech.

"It's cos you're not quite well, darlin'," said Froggy tenderly, answering back the look. "Don't try to say 'em no more to-night. Lie down, Benny, and I'll say 'em for you. Jesus'll take 'em just the same as if you said 'em, cos He knows you ain't well, and all about it !"

Benny lay down meekly as he was told, and then Froggy drew closer to him, and said his sweet baby prayers for him aloud, and repeated the hymn, "Gentle Jesus !"

Froggy's voice seemed to soothe Benny; he lay very still, listening, and after a time, Froggy noticed, with the quick eye of a watchful nurse, that a slight drowsiness was creeping over him, and that sleep was likely to come. In order not to break off the sounds that appeared to be lulling him, Froggy said another hymn when he had finished "Gentle Jesus !" which was one that he had learnt a long time ago, and which he remembered all but the first verse. He began at the second, which says :—

> " 'Tis good for boys and maidens
> Sweet hymns to Christ to sing,
> 'Tis meet that children's voices
> Should praise the children's King.
> For Jesus is salvation,
> And glory, grace, and rest,
> To babe and boy and maiden,
> The one Redeemer blest !

> " O boys, be strong in Jesus !
> To toil for Him is gain ;
> And Jesus wrought with Joseph,
> With chisel, saw, and plane ;

O maidens, live for Jesus,
Who was a maiden's Son;
Be patient, pure, and gentle,
And perfect grace begun !"

Benny was very nearly asleep now, and Froggy said the last verse very slowly and hushfully to complete the lullaby :—

" Soon in the Golden City
The boys and girls shall play;
And through the dazzling mansions
Rejoice in endless day;
O Christ, prepare Thy children,
With that triumphant throng
To pass the burnished portals,
And sing th' Eternal Song !"

"How 'appy that sounds!" murmured little Benny softly. " The boys and girls playin' in—the—Golden City"——and now almost as he spoke, his lips parted, his eyes closed, and he fell into a light slumber. Froggy waited a moment to make sure it was sleep; then he covered him up gently, and left the bedside.

Poor Froggy had had no dinner, and he was by this time ravenously hungry. Just to satisfy the cravings of hunger, he crept to the fire, and made himself a small basin of porridge; a very small one it was, because he was anxious to leave a large share of the oatmeal for Benny to-morrow. Then he crept to the stool, and sat down and ate it, silently and sorrowfully, as if he felt it to be a very lonely supper. He kept his eyes continually on the bed, in readiness

to jump up and run to him, if Benny made the
smallest sign. Now and then he murmured in his
sleep, and seemed to be waking; then Froggy said
softly, "Sh—sh—sh!" as mother did when he was
a baby, and soothed him off again!

It was a long time before Froggy got into bed,
he was so afraid of disturbing Benny. When at last
he did, he crept in as quietly as a mouse, and laid
himself down.

Two sadder little faces could not have been seen in
all London, I think, than the two lying side by side
on the pillow for the last time in the poor garret
to-night. The world's loneliness seemed to be there,
and poverty very deep, but ah! the two little brothers
were not really alone; they were not really poor!
For if our eyes could have pierced the darkness, we
should have known that there was watching over
them, that One who is the Light of the world, even
Jesus, in whose dear Presence there is an everlasting
assurance of joy and peace and fellowship.

Little children, pray for that Presence—pray that
Jesus may come and abide with you, then you can
never be very lonely, or very sad!

This night, there was a miserable yellow-haired
boy sobbing his heart out in a cell in one of the City
prisons, wishing that he had only kept honest and
true like Froggy and Benny, "tho' they was so
clemmed and hard-up." Yes! Mac had found out
his mistake at last. He had been feasting often,
while they had been starving, but the "reg'lar merry

life" had all come to an end now, and had brought him to what dishonesty and drunkenness will always bring a man or a boy, a woman or a girl sooner or later—degradation and despair !

CHAPTER XII.

THE PARISH DOCTOR.

HE next morning, Benny woke feverish and excited. His hair was wet on his forehead, and his eyes looked strained and unnatural, with a peculiar light in them. All night long he had been murmuring and gabbling in his sleep, throwing the clothes off him, and kicking Froggy, who was perpetually out on the floor, and creeping in again, but not minding in the least, "cos they was Benny's kicks!"

When morning dawned, and the light came in at the window, Froggy started up and looked at Benny wonderingly, for he did not look like Benny at all, but like some other little boy! And when Froggy spoke to him, and asked him how he felt, Benny sat up in bed, and began talking and stammering about horses and cats, and big rats and balloons, as if horses and cats, and big rats and balloons were pressing painfully upon his little brain, and he was trying to tell Froggy a long story about them. It was evident from the incoherent jumble, that Benny's mind was wandering, and that he must be worse, instead of better.

Froggy was so puzzled, that he went down and asked Mrs Blunt to come up and look at him. The charwoman came, and at once pronounced Benny to be in a very queer state.

"You must keep your brother as quiet as you just can, and try to amuse him," said she impressively to Froggy, after she had laid a hand on his burning forehead, and felt his feverish hands. " Mr Brown'll be here before long (Mr Brown was the parish doctor); he's acomin' early to see my Jemmy, who ain't as bright as he ought to be, and then I'll ask him to step up and take a look at Benny. He ain't well—no, that he ain't!" regarding Benny sorrowfully, and nodding her head.

"Please, mum, are you goin' out a charin' to-day?" inquired Froggy, full of that anxiety which seems so deeply implanted in men's breasts, to keep a woman in sight when there is sickness about.

"No, I ain't agoin' charin' to-day," said Mrs Blunt. "I'm goin' to be busy at my tub. Have you got anythink to make a fire with, Froggy?"

"No," said Froggy; "we've no sticks, nor yet coals."

Mrs Blunt answered nothing, but went downstairs. In a moment she returned with some coals and sticks out of her own little store, which she could ill spare, poor woman; but which, with the generosity of her class, she was so ready to give!

How many a beautiful lesson can we learn from the poor—for sufferings nobly endured and heavy burdens bravely borne, where can we look better than to them, but what *generosity* they teach us!' They show us how to be truly and greatly generous in their willingness to share the last crumb of comfort, whatever that may be, with a neighbour, kindly and ungrudgingly, without hope of return or reward. Theirs is not a generosity which costs them nothing —it often entails going without a meal or sitting by a fireless grate, but a self-sacrifice of some sort, *always.* It is of the highest and truest order, because the nearest to our great Pattern, whose generosity only reached its sublime perfection on the cross at Calvary, when the most perfect self-sacrifice was made that the world has ever known, and which nothing could go above or beyond! We are not called upon to lay down our lives, but we *are* called upon to make very great sacrifices, not only once, but daily and hourly, for one another; and in the homes of the poor, I think, we see this call answered as a rule more obediently and absolutely than anywhere else.

Mrs Blunt went down on her knees, and lit the fire for Froggy, out of sheer pity for his poor troubled face, that she guessed would soon be looking more troubled still. She had seen much of illness, and in this case something told her from the first that "God was going to call a little child" again, and that Froggy would shortly be alone, and brotherless. She bade him once more keep Benny quiet, and not to let

him talk; then having lighted the fire, and told
Froggy to give her a call if he wanted her, she went
downstairs to wait till the doctor came.

As soon as she was gone, Froggy took a seat
beside Benny, and began thinking what he could do to
amuse him, to carry out the charwoman's injunctions
to keep him quiet.

"Now, if you are a good boy and doesn't talk,"
said Froggy, "I'll tell you all about what I did out
yesterday"——

"The big rats"—began little Benny again on the
old theme, starting up and looking excited. But
Froggy interrupted him.

"You're not to talk," he said, putting up one finger
severely. "If you do, I sha'n't tell you nothink, Benny,
and you'll be a naughty boy!"

After this Benny kept still for some minutes,
gazing intently up at the ceiling, as if he saw something there which riveted his attention. Froggy commenced his narration of yesterday's doings, beginning
with his beautiful ride on the timber cart, and ending
with his interview with the tall soldier on guard at
Buckingham Palace. Benny was generally a delightful little fellow to tell a story to, so quick to take in
the smaller points, and so ready to laugh at all the
funny ones, and if there happened to be anything
about a *soldier* in it, Froggy had noticed that he was
generally doubly pleased and interested. Yes,
generally, but not to-day. He seemed too restless
and too feverish to listen, and though poor Froggy

laboured so hard to interest him, and to make him
laugh, he could not get Benny even to smile! This
struck more fear and apprehension into Froggy's
heart than anything else, I think; for Benny had
always been so merry; and there must be something
strangely wrong, argued Froggy, when Benny ceased
to laugh.   "Oh, that the doctor would make haste
and come!" that was his longing now, but it
was still so early, there was scarcely a chance of his
coming yet.

As a last resource, Froggy took to tumbling about
the garret in front of Benny, remembering how he
had laughed and clapped his hands that afternoon
when Mac came and tumbled previous to the Queen's
visit.   Though he had such a heavy heart, Froggy
went at the performance bravely, turning first the
most rapid somersaults one after another, then pausing
with a leg or an arm outstretched like a windmill in
the air, and his head on the ground, as if standing
upon it, or else in some other impossible position.   It
did not matter how daring or uncomfortable these
positions were; Froggy was not thinking of himself—
his one object was to try to astonish and amuse
Benny if he could, and to make him smile and clap
his hands, and be only as he used to be for a few
short minutes!

"Did you see *that?*" called out Froggy triumphantly from the floor once, after he had gone through
a series of acrobatic feats with such lightning
rapidity as to make him feel he had outdone himself,

and thinking that Benny would surely be sitting up, and laughing now. But there was not a smile on his little flushed face, as he stared at Froggy, and said—

"The balloon went up such a long way, Froggy, till the cat drawed it down!"—which made Froggy stare back, for what had this about the balloon and the cat to do with the tumbling? What was Benny talking about? Truly he was a very strange little brother to-day!

As he was regarding Benny with a puzzled air, Mrs Blunt entered the garret, and said gravely, "Still talking of cats and balloons! Poor Benny; he ain't much better then."

"If I could only make him laugh once again!" said poor Froggy mournfully.

"Well, p'r'aps Mr Brown'll be able—he's comin' up the stair now!" said Mrs Blunt kindly, and as she spoke, the heavy footstep which had so often excited Benny's hopes while little Deb was ill, came creaking up the stairs, and in another moment the parish doctor entered.

He was a very tall man, with a serious face and broad stooping shoulders, and a general air about him of being a hard worker. It was evident that with him, "Life was real; life was earnest!" and I who know him, children, can tell you that he was a worthy follower of that One who went about "healing all manner of sickness," and who has made, for all time, the calling of doctors so honourable and so beautiful!

L

I am anxious to pay here a tribute to doctors, for it seems to me that, as a class, they shine out more brilliantly than any other men. Their patience, their kindness, their zeal, their devotion, their courage—who has not proved it for themselves at some time or other in their lives, or else heard of it from others! How the poor invariably speak of them, and who better than they can testify to their real worth? I often think what a bright array of doctors there will be in that day, when all the great things done in the dark shall be known in the light, and the army of the world's true heroes shall appear before the great White Throne in heaven! How many a poor obscure country doctor, whose homely gig and hop-and-go-one horse have been the laugh and joke of the squire and his friends, when they have met him going his weary round on a sunny September morning, while they have been striding over the stubble with dog and gun, will be found in that day the better man of them all—amongst the little band "who are unknown here, but well-known *there!* " for deeds of gallantry and true heroism which this world passes by, but which will gain the highest honours and the brighest crown in the Paradise of God!

> "Where loyal hearts and true
> Stand ever in the light,
> All rapture through and through
> In God's most holy sight!"

The Doctor as he bent forward his head, and came in at the door of the garret, cast a rapid searching glance all around, as if he were struck by the cold and the misery and poverty of the scene upon which he had suddenly entered. He was accustomed to poverty and misery; he was in the habit of witnessing both the one and the other daily, in all its worst forms; hence, perhaps, his serious face, but *this* garret —well, it did strike him as being worse than anything he had seen for a long time! He followed Mrs Blunt at once to the little mattress whereon Benny lay, and beside which Froggy was standing.

Froggy gazed up anxiously into the doctor's face to see what sort of a gentleman he was; would he be kind to Benny? Would he be at all like that doctor who was so kind to him in the hospital? Dr Brown's very first words assured him on these points.

"How long has your little brother been ill?" he asked kindly, producing a very big watch, and taking Benny's tiny wrist to feel his pulse.

"Why, sir, since yesterday," said Froggy. "I come home from callin' at Buck'nam Palace at seven, and I finds him in a heap like on the floor, and when I raises him, he says, 'Froggy,' he ses, 'I thinks I got what the cab-horses has, the "staggers," and he couldn't stand up nohow! That was just how it all was, sir."

"And he's bin talking wild and strange ever since," put in Mrs Blunt standing by.

"Who takes care of you up here?" asked the doctor looking round.

"Please, sir, Benny and me takes care of ourselves," replied Froggy; "father and mother's both
dead, and we shifts along o' ourselves."

The doctor now asked many questions, to each
of which Froggy spoke up and answered promptly,
like a little soldier standing at attention. He told
the doctor all about the Punch and Judy show, how
mother had died, then how father had died, and how
very bad times had been ever since for Benny and
himself; lastly, of the letter they had written to the
Queen, and of how he had trudged over to Buckingham Palace yesterday, to see whether she had
got it, which brought him back again to his
coming home, and finding Benny in a heap on the
floor.

The doctor looked very grave over the story;
so grave that Mrs Blunt felt it due to herself to
explain that "she was out charing most days; had
a hard life of it herself to keep her own from the
workhouse, and hadn't much to give away, though
she had given what she could!"—which was all
true, poor woman.

"I only wish this had come to my knowledge
sooner," said Dr Brown; "there is little to be done
now, I am afraid."

"Couldn't you give him some medicine as 'ud do
him good?" cried Froggy imploringly, looking first
at Benny and then at the doctor, with great tears in
his eyes. "I ain't got the money to pay for it, but
I soon will have, and then I'll pay!"

"He's so fond of his brother!" murmured Mrs Blunt gently, for the doctor to hear.

"I will do all I can for him," said the doctor kindly, "and you need not trouble about the paying, my boy."

He closed his eyes for a moment, and Froggy felt sure he was praying. Yes—the doctor was a wise, Christian man, and he knew well enough that the physician's art would be all unavailing unless God's blessing was with him; so he just lifted his heart in prayer for one moment, that if it were God's will, the little sick boy now lying before him might be raised up again, but if not, that He would take care of Froggy, and comfort him exceedingly.

He then took out a pocket-book, and began writing on two pages, which he presently tore out and folded up. On one he put a large mark to distinguish it from the other.

"Now, my boy," said he to Froggy, "I want you to run with this to the chemist's in J—— Street," handing him the marked paper. "Leave it with the chemist, then run on to the red brick house next the church, in the same street, you know, ask for Mr Wallace, and give him this," handing him the other; "then, on your way back, call at the chemist's again, and he will give you some medicine. Do you understand, now, what I mean you to do?"

"Yes, sir," said Froggy, and he repeated his instructions over to show that he did.

"That is right," said Dr Brown, "now run, and we'll look after your brother while you're gone ! "

Froggy needed no urging. He clattered down the stairs, and ran out into the street in hot haste to do what the doctor had told him.

CHAPTER XIII.

"OH CALL MY BROTHER BACK AGAIN!"

AVING left the prescription at the chemist's shop, Froggy ran on to the red brick house next the church. He was on tiptoe, straining to reach the bell, which was rather high up, when a voice said behind him, "Good morning, little man—you needn't ring, I've got a key!" and turning round he saw that a gentleman in a black coat had gained the doorstep with him, and was just about reaching over his head to insert a small key into the hole.

"Where do you come from?" asked he, as he swung the door back on its hinges.

"I come from B—— Street to see Mr Wallis, sir," answered Froggy.

"I'm your man, then," said the gentleman. "I'm Mr Wallace. Come in, my boy—you look very cold."

Froggy followed the clergyman (for such he was) into a small room, rather bare of furniture, and with no carpet, but there was a bright fire burning, and a nice smell of hot coffee pervading the apartment, which gave it an atmosphere of comfort. A woman had just deposited, on the end of the square wooden table, a small tray, bearing Mr Wallace's simple breakfast of coffee and bread.

"The doctor said as I was to give you this, sir," said Froggy at once, handing him the paper.

The clergyman, as he took it, noted the sorrowful face of Froggy, and his own became very grave while he stood and read what the doctor had written to him, which was shortly this—"Dear Wallace, great misery in top attic, number 1 B—— Street. Case perhaps for Orphanage. Come as soon as you can. Yours, C. B."

He looked down kindly at Froggy after he had read the words, and said—

"Tell me a little about the trouble that is at home, my boy?"

"Please, sir,"——began Froggy, but that was all he could say. In another moment he was sobbing.

Mr Wallace, however, seemed to understand all about it; he had that "priestly gift of sympathy," without which, a good man has said, "we can never attain to the Christ-like distinction of being true sons of Consolation." It is a precious gift, rarely to be got except by going through very deep waters of suffering; those who have never suffered, can never have it as Christ loves to see it in His people.

"There, there," said Mr Wallace soothingly, laying his small gentleman-like hand on Froggy's little shoulder, "I've been through a perfect furnace of trouble myself, so I can feel for you."

"Did ever you have a little brother ill, and not know where to turn for bread?" asked Froggy, looking up with his streaming eyes.

"Not quite that, but something very like it," he answered. "I lost a little sister once when I was about your age, and later I lost other things which seemed to make me very poor till I saw God's hand was in it, and that He was leading me to happiness, though it was by a path I did not know. You've no father or mother?"

"No, sir," said Froggy; "Benny and me's quite alone."

While the clergyman had been speaking, he had poured out a cup of hot coffee which he now handed to Froggy.

"Here," said he, "drink this, little man. It will do you good."

"I'd rather not, sir—I couldn't wait, sir," said Froggy in a great hurry, drying his tears up with the sleeve of his jacket. "I must run back to Benny, sir; he'll be callin' for me."

"But drink the coffee first," urged Mr Wallace, "and you shall have the loaf to carry home to your little brother."

Froggy drank the coffee after this. The promise of the loaf made him feel he could take the coffee, since the bread would be an equivalent to Benny. It had been always so! Froggy could never enjoy a good thing unless Benny had his share of it!

"I shall be round to see you in less than a quarter

of an hour," said Mr Wallace kindly. "Stop one moment, though," he added, as Froggy, having finished the coffee and got the loaf, was about to run off.

"Tell me, isn't *Ragbon* the name of the person who keeps your house?"

"Yes, sir," answered Froggy. "That's she;—Sally Ragbon she's called."

Then, as he remembered what the landlady had said to the policeman about her dislike of "the long-coated gentry," he added quickly—

"But she don't like parsons, sir; she won't never let you in, I guess; she's terrible fierce."

"Oh, but she will have to do so, I shall insist," said the clergyman.

"She's awful strong!" said Froggy gravely. He looked at Mr Wallace measuringly, and thought he was not tall enough to grapple with such a giantess as Mrs Ragbon; but Froggy measured him wrongly.

Mr Wallace was a man of small stature, but with great breadth of shoulder, and a look of quiet, reserved power about him as if he could hold his own against any number of infuriated landladies.

Froggy had yet to learn that small men are quite as well able to grapple with strength, both morally and physically, as tall ones. It would have surprised him very much if you had told him, what is undoubtedly true, that some of the world's greatest warriors, who have led her armies to victory, have been quite small men, such as Napoleon, Wellington, and Havelock. Like Zaccheus of old, who, you remember, was small of stature, and triumphed over hindrances when he wanted to see Jesus, by climbing up into the sycamore tree, little men, as a rule, I think, overcome the obstacles and difficulties of daily life more determinedly and effectually and gallantly than taller men ; perhaps, because they are generally more strongly made, and are possessed of greater physical energy. I suppose Mr Wallace guessed what was passing in Froggy's mind, for he smiled and said—

"You think Mrs Ragbon is stronger than I am ? Well, we shall see shortly. In a few minutes I shall be round."

"Thank you, sir," said Froggy gratefully. And now with the loaf under his arm, and feeling all the better for the hot coffee, he left the friendly red brick house, and ran down the street to the chemist's again, according to the doctor's instructions. Having got the draught, he hastened home.

To his great surprise, when he reached the doorstep he found Mr Wallace already standing there (how true he had been to his word, and how very quick he had been over his breakfast!) in conversation with Mrs Ragbon, who had opened the door to him.

The landlady was actually smiling, and the clergyman was looking very pleasant, but resolute. Froggy heard her say as he came up—

"Please to walk in, then, your reverence. Here, Froggy," as she caught sight of him, "show his reverence the way." Froggy wondered why she was

so civil! The fact was, Mrs Ragbon had taken a
correct measurement of the small, square-shouldered
gentleman before her, and felt that he was quite as
determined to enter upon this occasion as ever she
could be to keep him out. There was, moreover,
another reason for her yielding to him, and yielding
pleasantly too. The policeman's visit lately, and
Mac's disgrace, had naturally brought her house into
great disrepute, and she thought it would look rather
well to the neighbours now, if they saw that she was
on terms with the clergy. I fear she had no higher
or better motives for behaving properly. Froggy led
the way, and Mr Wallace followed him up the steep
stairs to the garret, where Doctor Brown and Mrs
Blunt were still watching beside Benny. He looked
more flushed and excited than ever, as if he were
puzzling himself to comprehend who this strange,
tall gentleman was, sitting so close to him, and hush-
ing him when he talked. The doctor had got one
hand across his little chest, keeping the bedclothes
on him, for Benny was still restless and inclined to
kick them off.

As soon as Mr Wallace entered the garret, the
doctor rose up and met him. Their greeting, quiet
and undemonstrative, was evidently that of men who
were in the habit of meeting constantly, and between
whom there existed a perfectly good understanding.
Theirs was, indeed, no common friendship. Begun
as happy schoolboys on the play-ground at Win-
chester, and continued in all its warmth and freshness,

it had survived the wear and tear of years until now, when as men, we find them standing like faithful soldiers in the breach, "heart within and God o'er-head," working and fighting and striving together to stem the mighty tide of human misery and sin, which is everywhere abroad in this great city.

Froggy saw them shake hands and then begin to talk earnestly together with Mrs Blunt, but he did not wait to listen to what they said. He ran eagerly to the bedside, and showed Benny the bread.

"Look, darlin'!" he cried holding it aloft, "a beautiful loaf, crusty and hot, all for we!"

Such a sight had not been seen in the garret for many a day, but, alas! it had come too late for little Benny to enjoy. He took no notice, but asked if Froggy would soon be back?

"Why, Benny, he *is* back," said Froggy. "Look, Benny, 'ere he be—'ere's Froggy. I'm Froggy, don't you see, darlin'?" peering anxiously into his face.

"'Es bin away such a long while!" murmured Benny with a sigh, evidently not recognising his brother.

"He don't even know me now!" said Froggy sadly, as if this were the very climax of all his sorrows.

At this moment a friendly hand was laid on his shoulder, and Dr Brown's kind voice said—

"Don't lose heart, my little fellow, God has sent you friends at last; and now we are going to see what we can do for you!"

Looking up, Froggy saw that the doctor and the clergyman and Mrs Blunt had now drawn close to the bedside.

"I am going to send a lady to you," said Mr Wallace gently, "who will look after you, and nurse your little brother, and bring him all that he wants."

At the mention of a *lady*, Froggy felt disturbed. His thoughts instantly flew to the grand fly-a-way ladies, whom the boys chaffed in the streets, with large chignons and Grecian bends. How, thought he, would one of these do in the garret? But Mr Wallace's next words reassured him.

"She is a very kind, good lady," continued he, " accustomed to nursing and sickness, and she will do for your brother all that his mother would have done, if she had been alive. Miss Goff," he said, addressing himself to Mrs Blunt, "is one of the matrons of our Orphanage, so she will know exactly what to do in this case."

"Please, sir, when will she come?" asked Froggy.

"As soon as she is able—I'm going off to her at once," said Mr Wallace. " It may not be possible for her to come just yet. In the meanwhile, Mrs Blunt has promised to do all she can for you."

As he spoke, he slipped some money into the charwoman's hand.

"There, that will keep a good fire here and buy anything that is necessary till Miss Goff comes."

Mrs Blunt curtseyed and thanked him, and then they all quietly left the bedside, and went out on to

OH CALL MY BROTHER BACK AGAIN.

the landing, where they talked together for a few minutes in hushed tones. It was likely that Mr Wallace and the doctor were giving Mrs Blunt some last directions as to what she was to do for Benny, till the lady from the Orphanage came. Froggy heard them go downstairs, and then Mrs Blunt came back into the room with her face very grave and her eyes full of tears.

"Mrs Blunt," said Froggy, looking up into her face, "do you think Benny'll soon get well?"

"The doctor'll do all he can," said Mrs Blunt kindly, "but he's very ill, Froggy, very ill indeed. He's to have his draught now, and the doctor thinks that p'r'aps he'll go to sleep, and if he do fall off, Froggy, mind you're not on no account to wake him. We wants 'im to go to sleep—that's his best chance."

She poured the draught out into a mug, and brought it to the bedside. Froggy feared that Benny might object to it, as he had objected to his medicine yesterday; but to his surprise Benny sat up and drank it with avidity, for he was feverishly thirsty, and the draught felt cool and pleasant to his lips. This done, Mrs Blunt laid him down soothingly, and covered him over, telling Froggy to be sure to watch, and see that he did not throw himself about. "I shall be up and down," she said, the last thing, "to see how he's getting on, and I'm going to bring you something to eat, Froggy. The clergyman said he'd send some fresh meat in for us all to have a good dinner, God bless him!" Then she made up the fire, and went downstairs, leaving Froggy alone with his brother. We all know what it is, do not we? to be sitting by the bedside of some beloved one after a night or day of feverish tossing, and to be watching and praying for the blessed repose of sleep to come to them. How long it seems in coming, but when it does come, like many another good thing earnestly prayed for, and at last given, how unspeakably blessed it is!

It seemed a *very* long time to Froggy before Benny showed any signs of sleeping. He continued to murmur and to toss about as restlessly as ever, for some time, after Mrs Blunt left the garret, and Froggy was continually occupied in the hopeless task of keeping him covered up. But at last, at last! a delicious change came, something like the lulling of waters after a great storm; for Benny got suddenly quiet, and Froggy became aware that his eyelids had drooped, his lips were parting; and listening, his ear caught the sound of short, regular breathing. If nothing came to disturb him, he would assuredly be asleep in a few minutes. Froggy sat like a grave little sentinel beside him, holding his breath, and stirring neither hand nor foot, on very tenter-hooks lest something should break the happy spell. The street outside was full of turmoil and noise. There were costermongers with their barrows crying their cheap wares, dustmen going their rounds, calling out at intervals, "Dust ho-a, dust ho-a!" and cabs and

carts rattling past in a continual stream. And inside
the house, there were noises too. Now and then, a
door banged sharply, or a child screamed, or a lodger
called down to a neighbour below; there was never
anything of peace or repose in Mrs Ragbon's house.
At these sounds Benny sometimes stirred, but he did
not wake.

After a time Mrs Blunt came softly up the stairs
and put her head in at the door.

"Asleep?" she whispered.

"Yes," nodded Froggy.

Then she entered cautiously, and crept to the
bedside with a plate of meat and bread, which she
deposited on Froggy's lap.

"Eat it," she whispered, "it will do you good,
Froggy. It's fine butcher's meat."

She waited one moment with her eyes fixed stead-
fastly on Benny's face.

"Ain't he red?" said Froggy, following her eyes,
"and don't he look small, mum, and funny?"

"Bless him!" was all she could say, for the poor
mother was thinking of another little suffering face
that had lain looking just like his lately in the room
below; and it is possible that just then a vision arose
before her of two little playmates meeting on the
shores of a heavenly land, which filled her eyes with
tears, and blinded her for the moment. She turned
and poked up the fire; then she softly left the room.

Froggy sat with the plate on his lap for some time
after she was gone, looking down at it, but not eating.

M

By and by he took the bread and began munching it solemnly, but the meat he did not even taste. It would be so splendid for Benny, he thought, when he woke up, and cried for something to eat.

"He'll be ever so hungry, I guess, when he wakes," said Froggy to himself, and he stretched out one hand, and put the plate down noiselessly on the floor beside him.

As the morning wore on, and Benny still slept, an overpowering sense of fatigue came over poor Froggy. The walk to Buckingham Palace and back had been a long journey for him yesterday, and he had gone through anxiety and trouble enough since yesterday evening to try a strong man even, let alone a little weak, half-fed boy like himself! It was not to be wondered at, then, that he was worn out, and tired to a degree which bordered on pain. He did all he could to shake off the drowsiness which he felt was stealing over him; for if Benny woke and wanted something, what would Benny do if he (Froggy) were asleep? Every now and then his heavy lids would, in spite of himself, close over his weary eyes and compel him to doze for a few minutes, till, in a vague, dreamy, troubled sort of way he realised what he was doing; then he would start up, and open his eyes wider than ever, and stare fixedly at some object, till the same thing happened, and everything had to be done over again. By and by an organ came, and droned away in the next street, and Froggy began silently to follow the tune in his

own mind. He had heard the boys singing it in the
streets—

"When Johnny comes marching home !"

and the poor old organ seemed to be saying very
distinctly in its dull old voice, " Hurra ! hurra !" and
to be never tired of declaring—

"And—we'll—all—be—happy when—
Johnny comes marching home !"

Suddenly—Froggy found that he was drifting
away to the music of that tune ; that somehow .he
was in a boat, drifting out to sea, with Benny
standing on the shore beckoning to him. He tried
to drift back, but he could not, and away he floated
farther and farther, unconscious of everything except
that he was resting deeply, and that God was with
him in his little boat on the broad waters. Of course,
we know what had happened. Froggy had fallen
fast asleep, and was dreaming. Yes ! there he sat,
with his head bent forward, and his limbs dangling
limply from the old broken chair, in a deep heavy
slumber.

The day had grown a good deal older by the time
Froggy awoke. Dark shadows were creeping over
London, and reminding every poor toiler in the vast
city once again that—

"Be the day ever so long,
At length it ringeth to evensong."

The rough bawling cries of "Dust ho-a !" and cheap
vegetables of the morning had given place to those

of the water-cress and periwinkle sellers. The poor,
unhappy women whom all Londoners know so well,
were slipshodding along in woful garments, close to
the area railings, with their baskets hung loosely on
their arms, crying out in doleful trebles, "Any fine
water-cre-sees!" and the old men with their peri-
winkles, keeping up a sort of duet with their baser
cries of "Periwunks! periwunks!" were a sure sign
that four o'clock, the poor people's tea hour in the
East End, was nearly approaching.

Froggy woke himself with a long, deep-drawn sigh,
and would have rubbed his eyes, only that something seemed to prevent him from raising his hands.
Opening his eyes wide to make his vision clear, he
looked to see what was the impediment, and found, to
his surprise, that his body was packed up in a *shawl*
that was a total stranger to him. Whose shawl
could it be ? How had it come, who had brought it,
and who had packed him up like this ? wondered
Froggy, greatly amazed. It was not one of Mrs
Blunt's shawls. It was far too thick and good a
garment ever to have come out of *her* poor wardrobe,
of that he was sure ; but, then, whose could it be ?

He turned his eyes to the bed, and there, over
the tattered counterpane, was another strange wrap
spread, so as almost entirely to hide the small thin
body of Benny lying underneath. He began to
guess what had happened. The lady of whom Mr
Wallace had spoken must have come while he was
asleep and covered them up like this.

How soundly asleep he must have been, thought Froggy, never to have heard her! Was it not possible that Benny might have awakened and called for something, and not been able to make him hear ? .

Froggy felt keenly reproached when he thought of this, and it was with the greatest anxiety that he started up, and looked into Benny's face to discover what he could of his state. Froggy was relieved; things seemed very well with Benny now. The fever flush had left his cheek, and he was sleeping very quietly and calmly.

There is a superstition amongst Norwegian mothers that when children smile in their sleep, they are talking with angels. Well, these mothers would certainly have said that Benny was talking with angels now, for over his little thin white face there kept fleeting, as he slept, smiles so unexpected and happy, that Froggy began actually to smile too, out of sympathy! Froggy was on tiptoe, gazing wonderingly down upon him, when suddenly the small, peaceful face of Benny clouded over, the smiles all vanished, and his tiny bosom began to heave up and down with heart-breaking sobs. In another moment Benny was sitting up in bed with his arms clasped round Froggy's neck, crying as if his very heart were coming from him in tears. Froggy's distress was great.

"Whatever is the matter?" he said, clasping Benny tightly in his arms, and looking out with startled, troubled eyes at the wall. "What's the

matter, darlin'? what *is* the matter? Oh, I thought
you was well—I did think you was better, Benny!
Why, a minute ago you was laughing, and now you're
cryin' like this!"

"I 'ad—a—dream," sobbed Benny, "a beautiful—
'appy dream"—— but he could say no more.

"What was it all about, darlin'?" asked Froggy
rocking him to and fro. "It'll do you ever so much
good to tell me, that it will. I always told mother
whenever I 'ad a dream and didn't like it. Once I
thought she was drownded in the sea, and I woke
up a-cryin' just like you, and she comforted me ever
so, cos I told her just heverythink all about it!"

Benny now raised his head from Froggy's shoulder,
and without loosening his arms from about his neck,
he looked up into Froggy's face, and said in broken
whispers—

"Froggy darlin', I dreamt I was dead and gone
from here. I think I was in heaven, cos there was
angels, and all the little children's faces was bright,
and there was no tears. Nobody seemed hungry,
and nobody seemed thinkin' about their rent.
Little Deb was there, and she took me by the
hand, and we listened to the angels singin'. And we
went into fields and played,—and we was quite
happy till Deb said—she'd go and see her mudder,
and I said I'd—go and see you, Froggy! I come,
and I looked in at the window, and, O Froggy, you
was sitting all alone—in the dark cryin'!" and Benny
sobbed again as if his very heart would break at the

pitiful vision he had had in his dream of poor Froggy sitting alone and forlorn, with his head bowed in the empty garret, crying because he was dead.

"It was only a dream, you know, darlin'," said Froggy falteringly, clasping him very tight.

"Yes—yes!" murmured Benny, but he still continued to sob softly with that grievous, grievous pain with which we have all, God help us! awakened out of sleep sometimes after an intensely real and sorrowful dream.

The two little brothers remained locked in each other's arms for some minutes. At last Benny's sobs grew gradually less, and Froggy felt that by degrees Benny's little arms were loosening about his neck, as if he would shortly fall away from him.

"Benny, do you feels a bit comforted?" asked Froggy gently.

"Yes, Froggy, I can hear the angels singin' again!" said Benny faintly, and a peculiar light shone over his face. His hands unclasped, and he laid his little rough head back on the pillow. For a moment he was very still, then he said—

"Froggy—what's the time?"

"I've bin asleep, darlin', and don't know *quite*," said Froggy, "but I should think it's a'most four, cos the creesses is being called."

"Then it's near evening—everybody's going home," murmured little Benny, and Froggy heard him sigh deeply, but that was all! There was nothing else to tell that in London's sorrowful army of starving,

struggling people, another little sufferer had fallen out
of the ranks, because there seemed no room for it
here, and had gone with its pitiful face and bleeding
heart to lay its head down, and to be consoled and
comforted for ever more in the bosom of its Saviour !
A look of unspeakable rest and satisfaction settled on
his features, something that Froggy had never seen
before, though Froggy remembered it in his mother's
face after she was dead, and he thought Benny looked
very like mother now, though not so old !   He
stooped down and kissed Benny ; his face was very
cold ; he touched his hand and that was very cold
too.   He took the tiny limp hand between his own,
and rubbed it, but he could get no warmth into it.
How was it that Benny was so cold ?   But still Froggy
did not guess the truth.   He chafed the little hands
more vigorously, he spoke to Benny, he kissed him
again and again, at length he called to him, but he
did not answer.   Froggy grew uneasy, and was just
thinking he would call Mrs Blunt, when he heard
footsteps on the stairs.   Somebody was coming—
what a relief !   He would be able to tell them of this
strange deep sleep of Benny's.

A minute later the door opened, and two people
entered.   In the dusky light Froggy perceived that
one of them was Mrs Blunt, and the other was evidently the lady whom Mr. Wallace had said would
come.   She was tall and gentle looking, dressed in
quiet black clothes, and carried in her hand a basket
full of the food and necessaries, which she had dis-

covered were so sadly wanting when she had visited
the garret earlier in the day. She had found both
little boys asleep then, and (as Froggy guessed) had
covered them up softly with the wraps she had
brought with her; then she had left to fetch the
things with which she was laden now.

"Mrs Blunt," said Froggy in an anxious tone,
directly they appeared. "Benny's gone so dreadfully
asleep I can't wake him nohow, nor yet warm him
neither. Just you feel his hand, how cold it be!"

Both women hastened to the bedside; Mrs Blunt
with a look of grave apprehension on her face, as if
she feared what she might see. She took Benny's
chilly hand, and held it for a moment, but only for a
very brief moment. The first touch satisfied her of
what had happened, and she laid it down quietly,
from whence she had taken it, on the counterpane.
Miss Goff also took it, and without a word laid it
down in the same way. None of this world's heat,
they knew, would ever warm that little hand again;
none of its joys or sorrows bring either smiles or tears
to that little, still, white face on the pillow!

"Try and wake him!" said Froggy beseechingly,
as they turned and looked at him.

Miss Goff then drew him to her, and putting her
hand lovingly on his shoulder, she said with large
tears in her eyes—

"Froggy, your little brother is very happy, God
has made him so. You will not see him about any
more here, but in another world you will meet him,

and know him, and love him as your own little brother
again, and he will know you in heaven."

For a moment Froggy did not speak. He seemed
stunned and terrified.

" Can't we call 'im back?" he cried at last, "he
ain't bin gone long! he said he'd never leave me; he
said he'd be afraid to go that long journey all by hisself!—He's gone without nobody to look after him!
he said e'd never, *never* go without me!" and now,
poor little Froggy broke down and sobbed bitterly.

" He hasn't gone *alone*, Froggy," said Miss Goff
ever so tenderly, with her hand still touching him,
"God has been with him every step of the way.   He
would not suffer him to be either lonely or afraid;
oh, be quite sure of that!"

" If I'd only knowed he was goin', I'd 'a kissed 'im
more! I'd 'a said good-bye! I'd 'a told 'im more how
I loved 'im!" wept Froggy.   Then covering the little
dead body with frantic kisses, he sobbed, " O Benny!
Benny, come back! Benny, my brother—my dear
little brother—O my brother, come back! I can't live
without you, Benny! Benny! Benny!"

His words rang through the empty garret with a
wail of sadness, which struck painfully into the hearts
of the women standing by.

"You will not be left to live here alone," said Miss
Goff tenderly, " you must come home with me."

Froggy looked round the poor garret, where he
and Benny had been starving so long—the scene of
so many struggles, so many tears (but with all its

poverty it had a friendly home look to him) and he said mournfully, " Oh; let me stay ! "

" You'll be ever so comfortable, Froggy, if you goes with the lady," said Mrs Blunt.

" I don't wants to go anywhere comfortabler," wept Froggy. "If only Benny 'ud come back just once again, and speak to me. O Benny ! Benny !" he cried, "my dear little darling brother, come back ! Benny, come back ! "

It was vain to try and console him ; the same frantic cry went up for a long while after, and no entreaties, no persuasions would induce him to leave the bedside on which lay the cold, lifeless, little body of Benny. When at last his strength was thoroughly spent, and he could sob no more, he threw himself down on the bed which Mrs Blunt had prepared for him in a corner of the garret, and Miss Goff heard him murmur as he closed his eyes, " Mother said we was all to come by and by—and now all's gone— 'cept me ! "

So poor Froggy fell asleep. Miss Goff did not leave him. She knew what it would be to the broken-hearted little brother to wake up in the morning and face his sorrow alone, so she did an angel's work, and stayed with him all the night through, God bless her !

CHAPTER XIV.

FROGGY COMFORTED.

NEED not tell you how sorely Froggy cried when the day came for Benny to be laid in his coffin, and carried to the grave. When he kissed his little brother for the very last time, and looked upon his meek white face, and whispered to him his last passionate appeal to wake up before they came to carry him away, his grief was such that I care not to dwell upon it.

The funeral was much like little Deb's, only that there were not so many followers. Benny had no mother to weep for him, and no sisters; Froggy was his chief and only mourner. Miss Goff came very early in the morning, and when it was time took Froggy by the hand and followed with him through the maze of busy streets, out to the quiet cemetery, where so many tired citizens had entered into their rest. There were no butter-cups and daisies yet, but the little spring flowers were beginning to come up, and in the stillness and solitude about the silent graves, there seemed to be the Shepherd's voice sound-

ing over all, reminding the poor mourners who came
to weep there, of that sweet and most consoling
promise, "And they shall be Mine, saith the Lord, in
that day when I shall make up My jewels."

When all was over, Miss Goff took Froggy by the
hand again and led him back to Shoreditch. Not to
the old house with the blackened front, but to a large,
clean, red brick one, standing near to the church, with
the words printed over the door, in large letters,
"Suffer the little children to come unto Me."

This was the Orphanage of which Miss Goff was
under-matron, and where Mr Wallace had arranged
that Froggy should be sheltered for a time, till another
home could be provided for him. There were twelve
little children, altogether, in the Orphanage. Very
noisy and very happy seemingly, but poor Froggy
felt strangely sad and lonely amongst them. He was
very quiet and tearless after the funeral, doing all
that was told him, and being a good little boy, but
not joining in the children's games, or laughing with
the rest. He was too sad to do that for many a day
after Benny's death.

You will like to know what became of poor little
Froggy, will you not? Well, he was removed from
the Orphanage shortly, and sent, through the kindness of Dr Brown and Mr Wallace, to a Home for
little boys in the city, where he is learning the trade
of a carpenter. I must tell you of something which
happened soon after Froggy entered the Home.

One winter's night, near Christmas time, Mr Wallace

and several gentlemen of the Committee were busy
at the Home auditing the accounts, and looking into
the many matters which required their attention at
this season of the year. They were seated round a
wooden table, a gas burner overhead, and a roaring
fire in the grate; in a small room off a much larger
one, also gas-lit and warmed, where there were a
number of boys (inmates of the Home) of all sizes
and ages, of all kinds and descriptions to be seen.
It was a bitterly cold night outside; the snow lay
thick on the ground, clean and compact like the
sugar on the top of a bride-cake, without an appearance of thawing, and everybody knew it was freezing
still. Skating had been going on all day in the
parks, and boys and men muffled-up to their chins,
were returning brisk and joyous from the ice, confident they would have another good day upon it,
to-morrow. How sharp the air was, and how the
voices seemed to ring out when there was talking in
the streets! It was well to be indoors on such a
night!

Mr Wallace was sitting with a very grave face cast-
ing up accounts, and the other gentlemen were very
busy too, when they were interrupted by the porter
coming in and addressing Mr Wallace.

"Please, sir," he said, "there's a policeman outside
wants to see you."

"A policeman!" repeated the clergyman looking
up. "Do you know his business at all?"

"No, sir," said the man. "He's got something

carrying in his arms, but he didn't say what it was."

Mr Wallace looked a little worried, but quietly laid down his pen and went out into the hall, from which he presently returned looking very thoughtful, and somewhat anxious.

"Well, Wallace, what is it?" asked the gentlemen.

"Shall I call in the policeman and let you see?" said Mr Wallace.

"Yes," said the gentlemen of the Committee. "Let the policeman come in."

There was a profound sensation in the larger room amongst the youthful inmates of the Home, when a moment later a very tall policeman entered, covered with snowflakes, carrying under his wet oilskin cape a bundle, from which hung down a small bare leg and a little boot. It was a bundle with a voice, for they heard it distinctly crying; and excitement rose to a very high pitch, as the guardian of the public peace carried it solemnly through the crowd of boys into the room where Mr Wallace and the gentlemen of the Committee were waiting. The boys followed the policeman eagerly, and pressed close up to the door of the Committee room, which was left open behind him. Foremost amongst them was our little friend Froggy.

The policeman's story was soon told. An accident had happened on his beat, a very short distance from the Home; a poor working man carrying a little boy in his arms, had been knocked down by a runaway horse, and taken off insensible to the hospital. The child crying piteously, and terrified almost to death, had been left to the tender mercies of the crowd, till Police Constable 27 X appeared upon the scene, and took him under his wing to the Police Station.

"What have you found out about him, policeman?" asked one of the Committee.

"Well, all I can get out from him, sir," said the policeman smiling, "is, that his name is Billy, and that he lives upstairs with father, and has no mammy. Where he lives, or who he is, we shan't know, sir, till the father comes to himself in the hospital and tells us. Poor little chap!" he said kindly, looking down under his cape from which little sobs had been audible all the time, "he seemed quite cowed at our Station. The Inspector sent me on here with him. Billy, speak up now, and tell the gentlemen who you are!" and the policeman exhibited him to the Committee.

Unless there had been such trouble in the matter, I am sure that at this stage of the proceedings the gentlemen would all have laughed; as it was, a very amused look came into more than one countenance, and exclamations of, "Oh my!" "Oh lor'!" "What a little rum 'un!" came distinctly from the group of boys peeping in and pressing up against the open door.

Billy was the tiniest thing in the shape of a boy you ever saw, and quite one of the funniest! He

" A moment later a very tall policeman entered, covered with snowflakes,
carrying under his wet oilskin cape a bundle, from which hung down a small
bare leg and a little boot."

Page 191.

had a small pinched face, with a very red nose, and bright little black eyes, which, in the gaslight, he blinked very much. He sat up in the policeman's arms and eyed the gentlemen very keenly for a few moments, as if he were anxious to take in their respective characters; then having satisfied himself apparently that no one was going to hurt him, he amused and astonished them all exceedingly, the stolid policeman into the bargain, by suddenly diving into his pocket, producing a nut, and quietly cracking it with a precision that showed Billy had got some good strong teeth of his own. He proceeded to eat it, taking very small bites at a time, much after the fashion of marmozet monkeys in the Zoological Gardens, and regarding the amused faces around him with a gravity that was truly comical.

"Are you hungry, Billy ?" asked the policeman, giving him a little shake.

Billy vouchsafed no answer, but went on munching the nut.

"What's to be done with him, Wallace ?" inquired the chairman laughing. " He seems wide awake to the charms of a nut, doesn't he ? "

" Yes," said Mr Wallace, regarding him thoughtfully; "he's too small for the Home, I am afraid. How old are you, Billy ? "

Billy either did not know, or he thought this a rude question, for he gave no answer.

"Not more than four or five, I should think," said Mr Wallace. " How the light and the warmth are

N

reviving him! We had better call Mrs Holt, and hear what she says."

Mrs Holt was the matron of the Home; a kind, motherly person, whose heart went out in compassion at once to the unfortunate little waif in the policeman's arms. But she gave it as her decided opinion that he was too young for the Home.

" You see he's really not much more than a baby," she said, addressing the Committee. " And there's not a single bed vacant, gentlemen, in the house."

" Then I shall have to take him to the Union," said the policeman preparing to wrap him up again in his cape, and to face the cold and the snow once more. Whereupon Billy uttered a little wail, and called out—

" Oh, please, don't take Billy out in cold again!" with an appealing look at the gentlemen, as if he thought they could not possibly countenance such an act of barbarity.

" It does seem hard to turn him out on a night like this," said the chairman. " Wait a moment, policeman. Mrs Holt, is there, indeed, no corner you could put him in? You see he's not very big."

" No, I's quite little," wailed Billy, showing that he understood very well what was said.

" Indeed, sir, every bed is full," declared the matron, " Unless we were to put him in with one of the boys"——

Before she had time to finish her sentence a movement was heard amongst the eager, listening group at the door, and in rushed Froggy, his face quite quivering with excitement. Unmindful of the many eyes that were instantly turned upon him, he stood before the Commitee, the matron and the policeman, and made quite a passionate appeal on Billy's behalf.

"Let *me* take him! let *me* take him!" he cried. "Give him to me; don't turn him away! he shall have half my bed, half my supper, half my clothes, half everythink I have, but don't turn him away! He's like Benny, sir, somethink like Benny, ain't he?" turning with earnest, streaming eyes to Mr Wallace, the only one present who had known his little brother.

"Yes, Froggy, something like, certainly," said Mr Wallace, laying his hand kindly on Froggy's shoulder, as if to calm his excitement; then Mr Wallace turned to his friends, and in a few graphic sentences told them what he knew of Froggy and of Froggy's little brother.

The story seemed to touch them greatly. One kind old gentleman began clearing his throat, as if he were going to speak, but he could not get out a word. Another took off his glasses and began polishing them vigorously, as if they had become suddenly dimmed, which was really the case.

"Well, now, let us consider," resumed Mr Wallace. "Mrs Holt, what do you say to this arrangement; could Billy be put in with Froggy to-night, do you think?"

"Well, sir," said Mrs Holt, "Froggy's a good boy,

and if he'll promise to help me with him, we *might*
manage it just for to-night."

"Or say till after Christmas," said the kind old
gentleman, who had recovered his voice. "I'll double
my subscription, and I know others," looking at some
benevolent gentlemen with whom he had been con-
ferring, "will do the same in order to keep Billy in
the Home for a time. Eh, Mrs Holt?"

Mrs Holt, nothing loth to give shelter to one more
helpless little soul, cheerfully agreed, and the policeman was just about to hand him over to her when
Froggy coming close up, stretched up his arms
towards Billy, and said—

"Oh, please, sir, let me take 'im! come to me, darlin',
won't you?" speaking to him as he used to speak to
Benny. "I'll cuddle you up ever so warm in my nice
little warm bed, and give you half my supper, Billy,
and never let anybody hurt you, Billy, never, never!"
And Billy, with a curious look of newly-awakened
interest and satisfaction in his face, held out both his
hands so as to clasp Froggy's, and showed unmistak-
ably that he was going to take very heartily to his
new-found protector and friend.

The last thing Mrs Holt saw that night when
going her rounds through the quiet dormitories after
everything was still and hushed in the Home, was
little Billy fast asleep on Froggy's pillow, and Froggy
sitting up in bed looking down with the intensest
interest and delight on his funny little bedfellow.

"Are you very happy, Froggy," inquired the

matron, as she paused for a moment with the light in her hand. " Is there room for you both in your little bed ? "

" Oh yes, mum," answered Froggy. " Plenty." And then she noticed there were big tears falling down his cheeks, as he said, " He *is* like my darling little brother Benny somethink ; I'm sure he is ! "

" Would you like to call him *Benny*, Froggy ? " asked the matron kindly.

" Oh no, no, *no,*" said Froggy, " I couldn't never do that ! There'll never be another Benny again, *never !* But I think Billy's a bit like 'im, I do think that really, and I'll be ever so good to 'im, mum—for Benny's sake, that I will. You don't think the gentlemen'll turn him out after Christmas, does you, mum ? "

" Well, I can't say—we shall see," said Mrs Holt soothingly. " Good-night, Froggy," and she passed on.

The policeman called at the Home next morning, to say that Billy's father had died during the night in hospital, from injuries received, without having recovered consciousness. So now Billy was an orphan and destitute. The kind gentlemen of the Committee still keep him in the Home, and the last thing I heard of Froggy and Billy was, that they, with several other pale-faced, sorrowful-eyed little boys, were wondering anxiously whether enough money would come into the Home this year to give them a treat in the country ! The other boys had one last year, and, oh, what a day it was ! Tea in a hay-field, and games afterwards, and *such* a ride through the city in decorated vans. The smell of the hay, and the singing of the birds, and the shouts of their play-fellows visited them in their dreams long afterwards, and quickens their comprehensions still, when on Sunday they are talked to of the love of God, and the beauty of all His works. Better than all the sermons and books in the world, will a day in the country teach them of these.

Parents and little children, you especially who are rich, remember it is the Froggys and Bennys of London for whom your clergyman is pleading, when he asks you to send money and relief to the poor East End! They may be street Arabs, but they have immortal souls, and they are our brothers and sisters, though we may not own them. As we hope to partake of the same citizenship in the one Ever-lasting City, let us take care how we disregard our pastor's pleading, for when we are arraigned at the Last Day before the Judgment Seat of Christ, and Christ asks us, "What have you done for my little ones?" the excuse, "Lord, we never knew any!" will avail us little with Him, Who made His King-dom above all a children's Kingdom, and Who will hold us responsible for the little souls that enter into His Presence there, maimed and scarred and ignorant for the want of the care, and love and teaching, which we on earth have denied them.

We may not from circumstances be able to go and labour personally amongst them, but we can help those who are, and there are so many ways of doing it! all through the year by sending our pennies and shillings to help schools, and Homes, and Kindergartens for their benefit. In summer time by responding liberally to the appeals made through the Press and other channels for funds to enable poor little East End children to have a day in the country; and at happy Christmas time, when appeals are made for warm clothing and Christmas dinners. Let us not be dismayed nor discouraged by the apparent smallness of the returns for what we do; if we cannot *cure* the sorrow and the sin, we may at least mitigate them, and are we not told to "sow in faith beside all waters?" Let us be content to wait for our reward till that Day when the truth of the saying, "Cast thy bread upon the waters, and thou shalt find it after many days," shall be manifested to us, as, doubt not, O rich man, it *shall* be manifested, wonderfully, fully, overflowingly, with the same Divine generosity which made the lame man not only to walk, but to leap; the wine at the wedding in Cana of Galilee to be *more* than enough; and the very fragments of the miraculous feast to be twelve baskets *full!*

THE END.

Lightning Source UK Ltd.
Milton Keynes UK
UKOW031808190912

199292UK00001B/53/P